NEURO CONFINEMENT

Rage Against the Dream

Sophie Marie White

Absolute Author Publishing House

New Orleans, La 7012

Absolute Author
Publishing House

Neuro Confinement
Copyright© 2019
Sophie Marie White

Publisher: Absolute Author Publishing House
Project Editor: Dr. Melissa Caudle
Line Editor: Rory White
Graphics, Cover and Back Page: Rebecca from RebeccaCovers
Author Photographer: Selfie of Author

Library of Congress Cataloging-in-Publication Data

Wright, Sophia.
    Neuro Confinement/ Sophia Marie White
        p. cm.
ISBN: 978-1-7337182-3-3

    1. Thriller   2. Suspense

0 1 2 3 4 5 6 7 8 9

Printed in the United States of America

ABOUT NEURO CONFINEMENT

Imagine a drug that imprisons convicts inside their minds where seconds turn into days and days into years.

NEURO CONFINEMENT is a Sci-Fi thriller, written by Sophie Marie White. A young idealistic scientist, Dr. Casey Palmer, developed a revolutionary new drug, D-214, that imprisons convicts inside their minds. His discovery promised to replace the skyrocketing incarceration problem by shortening sentences. One day in Neuro Confinement equals one year, whereas a thirty-year sentence is served in thirty days saving the penal system hundreds of billions of dollars. There is one major side effect -- users experience a living, breathing, Daliesque world, where side effects such as psychotic breaks and violent rampages erupt hours to years after the drug has been administered. Will this new wonder drug be the savior of the American penal system? Or, will prisoners be trapped eternally in their minds forever?

DEDICATION

I dedicate this book to my best friend of thirty years, Romaine. Thanks for being my rock and for putting up with my early writing that no one could read, along with my endless drafts. Your strength and dedication have taught me more about love than I thought possible. Thanks for saying, "Yes," all those years ago and changing my life. I love you more now than ever.

Thanks for everything.
Thanks for being there
when I needed someone.

Love you

Sophie Marie White

ACKNOWLEDGMENT

My first novel would not have been possible without several people. My heartfelt thanks to my two writing mentors, Hal Croasmun, and Wayne Pere.

Others who played a big part in helping shape this novel were my Screenwriting U compadres Delia Colvin, Tracee Beebe, Vicki Posidis, Jahn Westbrook, Cheryl Croasmun and the rest of the gang including MSC 4, 9, and 10.

I want to thank my friends, John Schnieder, John Swider, and Pedro Lucero, who provided feedback to me on the screenplay and the initial draft of this book.

To my editor, Dr. Melissa Caudle, I am eternally grateful for her guidance and expertise in all things publishing a book and guiding me through the steps. Also, for just being my friend and accepting me unconditionally.

To Dr. Carol Michaels, from Absolute Author Publishing House, for taking on my book.

To my book cover designer, Rebecca from Rebeccacovers, thank you for carrying out my initial vision. You are a true artist in every sense.

TABLE OF CONTENTS

CHAPTER ONE

The Monster Inside

Most scientists probably started their careers with noble intentions. I know, I did. Yet, life tainted those intentions, throwing things at me, I never even dreamed -- because, that's life. For me, it all started twenty-five years ago when a three-time convicted felon visited my family and took my daughter, Julie, from me. She was the one thing I had left that made my life still worthwhile. After that, my heart turned stone-cold and hardened. Revenge became my elixir and my motivation, which drove me toward the brink. That murderous felon tore my family apart, turning me into a hideous monster in the process.

I always thought I was the good guy in my scenario, which I call my life, but I turned into a facsimile of Dr. Jekyll and Mr. Hyde and forced with difficulty to accept the new me -- the me whom a weak person should become terrified once they got to know me.

1

"Vengeance is mine," said the Lord. I thought I would help Him. The wrath of the Lord is might, and mine could easily match when provoked. We share at least one thing in common.

It's incredible the amount of damage a cold-dead heart can do to your soul. My rage for revenge became my burning desire and my sole purpose to remain in this world. It was my elixir and motivation. I convinced myself that I was involved in fixing one of society's misfortunate ills; but if truth be told, I plotted a way to turn my nightmares into the criminals' other lives. A tricky process I might add, but I was up to the challenge.

My goal was to put convicts through the level of Hell, they caused me, but multiplied by ten thousand times having no escape plan. When they heard my name, I wanted to make sure they trembled as I consumed their thoughts, dreams, and controlled their eternity; their new manifested reality deemed as a punishment to fit their crimes.

You could go as far as to say I was pissed -- immensely angered. I knew I was righteous and noble and didn't care how they saw me only if they never forgot the pain they caused. More importantly, they lived in torment as I had for years, never knowing what was around the next corner. I was steadfast in my resolve to make sure they experienced a living Hell -- a Hell more than my Hell. The demon in me was deep-seated and formidable, and I worshiped it.

My name is Dr. Casey Palmer. I have a degree from one of the most prestigious Ivy League schools in the Northeast, and I am a scientific researcher. However, instead of listing my accolades and accomplishments, this tale began with one of my first failures. I must confess that describing it would not do it justice; so, I present it to you in their own words and thoughts as I shared them inside Neuro Confinement.

In case you're wondering, I can reveal my patients' hopes, fears, and especially their nightmares because they were one of my bestowed curses having invented Neuro Confinement. You see, I shared his thoughts living with them as if I were him. I don't mind his Hell if I get to exact my revenge. Revenge was sweet, and I tasted it.

I would tell you his words, but it's more complicated than that. Those words were our words as we lived them together linked inside of Neuro Confinement. It became more difficult each hour to separate our thoughts as we merged in the vacuum of a faux eternity. We linked, we merged, we thought like one. I told you it was complicated.

I wondered if my patients had the ability as I did when I connected my thoughts to theirs. Then again, I was always the smarter one as the inventor of D-214.

Sometimes I questioned my sanity because I couldn't determine whose thoughts emerged. Mine? His? Theirs? Some were alarming as my life had turned into my Hell on earth, but more on that later. Welcome to the first merge in Neuro Confinement with Rico Rodriguez, a thirty-year-old psychotic criminal.

***

Oh, what a sight the city was at dusk where the dirt and grime seemed like the only thing which kept this godforsaken, rat-infested, granite and concrete hellhole together. Just four months since my last departure and this place appeared to have aged thirty horrific years. The sun gradually set behind the buildings turning the streets a dingy urban pallet that caused the strongest of men to become uneasy.

The mercury vapor lights popped on as daylight faded into darkness. A sign read -- "Central Avenue Plaza."

Everywhere Rico gazed there were bums in full force on this dismal evening. *Why is everyone in a hustle? Don't they know they could slow down?* Hustling through the streets wasn't Rico's game. From my point of view, he only wanted one thing -- quiet. He relinquished to the fact that his perfect environment included silence, and no light -- just darkness and quiet because he screamed as loud as he could. Regardless, I made zero noise inside of his Neuro Confinement as a hellhole observer.

Rico Rodriguez was young, yet he looked seventy, and his mind a hollow shell having been broken by his Neuro Confinement. His mind continually raced; it never stopped, not even when he slept. That was one part of Neuro Confinement hell.

My biggest problem was that I couldn't discern reality from his illusion. The doctors did a real mind fuck on the both of us. Rico took the easy way out; or, so he thought. He was confident that if he could do it over, he'd take the thirty years in prison over what I gave him to enter Neuro Confinement. At this point, all he knew was that he fucked up!

Two days passed, but he needed more time to adjust to his unique environment. If he could only slow his mind down, stop it from racing, thinking, and analyzing every outcome, his outcome would be different. Each 'What if' scenario remained locked inside his head and gurgled with no escape multiplying and pounding deeper as they piled higher and higher taking up more of his quiet space. It elevated to the degree that the process drove him insane.

He turned to look at his wife, Magee, who once thought Rico was handsome, but now she believed that he was a monster. She was correct, and I knew he was. She enjoyed hanging on him even though he couldn't respond. Her warm gaze won't warm his now stone-cold cavern, which used to house his heart. Neuro Confinement destroyed him.

In this place, there were only right and wrong -- no more gray areas. Good and evil persisted as the way of life which sounded right at least. Wasn't there always the good versus the sinister?

Rico balanced his wife's goodness; therefore, I concluded that he was evil. In fact, eviller than you could imagine and didn't want to know. She tightly held onto him as we headed toward the subway entrance.

She dragged Julio, their six-year-old son -- the only good thing he ever produced from his loin. She held him firmly and reassuringly as a large burly man stepped in front of them.

The stranger pierced his eyes, narrowing his thick brows. "Hey, you have an extra smoke?" His voice as gruff as his burliness seemed threatening, and I witnessed the fright on Rico's family's faces. It was as if I saw their blood pulsate in their wrists and necks. Veins across their forehead often bulged.

Rico's mind raced, and his heart thrummed against his ribcage as if it tried to escape. He didn't recognize the burly stranger and owed him nothing. Why was he blocking their path? Did he want a cig? Did he want more than that? Rico wondered if he made a move toward him, would he jump out of the way or kill him? His eyes darted toward the trash can. No, the trash can was too heavy for a weapon. *If I were Rico, would I run? Fight? Kick? Punch? Kill!*

I felt Rico's every thought. That's what I did; I analyzed every single outcome possible on the face of the earth. Would I bite off his ear? Would Rico? Would I jab my thumbs through his eye sockets? Would Rico? Would I use my key card that made a nasty cut when appropriately held like a knife? Would I use my bare hands? Would Rico?

I made up my mind what I must do to survive and cope if it fell within the black-and-white guidelines set by the masters who controlled Neuro Confinement. The looming question was what Rico would do?

As I analyzed everything, I felt a sharp, disturbing pain inside my skull. My brain felt as if hit with a brain freeze. I placed my hands onto my temples and pushed, hoping to thaw whatever caused the pain. It helped somewhat, but not much, barely if anything. The pain remained pressing on my brain. When I looked up, Rico experienced the same thing, and I knew it.

Magee noticed; she tried to help him. "Rico, are you okay?" The urgency in her voice alerted Rico that he looked strained and anguished. No, make that agony for him.

Even the burly guy became concerned as he lifted his bushy unkempt brows. "Hey man, you, all right?"

Rico, gripping his hair, stumbled toward the stairs. "I need to get home." The dark void in front of him seemed to call him as he stammered toward it.

I need quiet darkness and sooner rather than later. Rico grabbed his hair and tugged harder.

A slow sigh escaped from him as he toppled onto the subway station platform and listened to the roar of the train headed toward him. His mind relaxed, but only slightly and barely noticeable to me. He offered zero explanation as to why the subway cars' roar quieted his mind tying it all together like a symphony of mindless chatter which caught up with my racing mind.

A deafening-squealing and high-pitched alarm sounded. Rico immediately became alert and scanned the area for problems and workable solutions. He realized as stragglers squeezed into the subway car, the sound was only a warning that the subway car's doors would close in five seconds. I wondered if they were fleeing from me, not Rico because they knew who and what I was and what I could manipulate to my vengeful cravings.

As my thoughts slowed, I realized it was only rush-hour traffic, and the train door's closed. It had nothing to do with me, per se. Within seconds the train barreled out of the station pulling with it my symphony of relief. As it left, the station quietened, and the pain crept back in as a dull throbbing ache.

Magee, Julio, and Rico remained on the platform as the subway train made the corner thundering out of sight.

Rico spotted a quiet and somewhat isolated bench away from the main traffic area. He knew he needed time to regroup his thoughts to stop his world from proceeding. When surrounded by confusion and noise, complete silence proved the cure to his mind's haunting.

There was one other thing that could stop or silence Rico's brain from pounding beside the subway roar. He reached inside his pocket for a bottle of ibuprofen which the prison psychiatrist prescribed. *Seriously, take four every six hours*. He never understood his pain as the first hour passed with negative zero relief.

Rico dashed out another six of the white-small pills, and dry swallowed them. As expected, they only slightly took the edge off. The pain never went away and was a constant reminder of his thirty years of Hell spent in just thirty days of real-time. It became increasingly difficult to tell the difference between real-time and *mind* time because there was none for the both of us.

Magee felt she couldn't snuggle close enough to him. Rico just sat motionless with his mind racing, and his head throbbed in agony. His mind went back to the cigarette guy. He couldn't shake him. What if he wanted something else, something more, how could he stop him? *Will these thoughts ever slow down? I guess I should know that answer?* At this moment, death seemed like the perfect solution, but whose death. Mine? Rico's? The stranger? His wife? His son?

Rico produced several 'What if' scenarios which tormented both of our minds. *What if the cigarette guy came down here? How could I protect myself? Could I protect my wife? What about Julio? Oh God, what if he wanted Julio?* That thought terrified him because Rico couldn't ever let a stranger take his child because he would kill him first. I easily identified with him.

He needed a course of action. *What is near? What is handy? What can I use to defend myself? What if? What if? Fuck!*

Magee wanted to give him another hug, and she tried to hold him tight. Her embrace temporarily shifted his focus away from his torture. She tried to be reassuring because she wanted her family back. That meant she wanted Rico back too.

Rico questioned her sanity now. They were never one since the beginning, so why would she want him back? I never could wrap my head around that one either.

Julio was the doppelganger of a vibrant Rico. Julio used to make him smile by gazing at him, but now he didn't give him a reason to smile, which worried him more. He did miss his smile. What if he smiled again? Would he enjoy it as much as he missed it? There went the what if questions again. *What if? What if? What if? Fuck, what if!*

We were at the end of the corridor. That was as far away as we could get from the rush-hour crowd. Rico's precious son sat on the ground next to them playing. He was a good kid. Rico hoped he didn't pass any of his evil traits to him. *Have I corrupted him yet? Does he take after me? Does he think about killing someone? I think not, but how can I be sure? Was there a way to tell? Will he snap like me, or will it be a slow progression that will gnaw away at his soul a little at a time as he grows older?*

Julio was oblivious to Rico's thoughts. Rico guessed he should be thankful for that but wasn't. He only stated the facts. His son played with his toy truck creating a battering ram against two green toy army soldiers. Rico was determined to shield him from everything evil. He knew he would have to protect him no matter the cost. This was his only job now -- to keep Julio pure and to keep evil away.

Rico rejoiced in the smile Magee flashed him, but it didn't last long. Her lips formed a beautiful heart shape. She took a deep breath. "I can't believe it's already been a month."

He nodded and returned and thin-lipped grin. "For me, it has been years, more like thirty, to be exact!"

I counted the days -- ten thousand, nine hundred, and fifty-two. I counted them off every day. It was part of my ritual. The only problem in Neuro Confinement was day and night never existed. It was all the same. So, I wasn't sure, but my bones could tell the mileage I was getting by joining in Rico's Neuro Confinement.

Magee smiled, and she hugged Rico again. Her warmth was pleasant, but Rico couldn't have anything nice because he always turned it into something evil. He must keep evil at bay at all cost before it consumed them.

Rico shivered. *Wait! The cigarette guy. What did I do to stop him? Why didn't he come after us? Is it because I put my hands on my head? I don't think so, but then again, maybe. I'm not sure. Perhaps I did. Perhaps I didn't.*

How many times would Rico ask himself this before his mind exploded? These thoughts wouldn't stop regularly racing through his mind. Nothing could stop those, not even slow them down. All of them kept playing and repeatedly playing as if his brain was about to overload.

Julio played with intensity as he shoved the toy truck toward the subway tracks. The truck scooted across the ground, clipping the metal edge of the curb flipping bumper to bumper and ultimately crashing onto the subway tracks below. Julio quickly looked toward his parents, but they weren't paying enough attention. He looked back at the rails.

"I'm so glad you took the program." Magee slid her hand down Rico's arm. "I'm not sure if I could have lasted thirty years without you."

"My dear Magee." All emotions slid from Rico's face as his demeanor became cold; all he could do was stare frozen in fear of what that program was, is, might be.

What would it continue to do to me? How much had it fucked with my mind? That is, what little amount of my mind I have left.

10

Rico couldn't explain how much of a Hell he experienced in the last thirty years even though it was only a month of real-time; he didn't believe it. He couldn't, and he found me repeating his thoughts. *Was that real? Did I live for thirty years? Where is my mind now?*

I was left with one conclusion -- it was a side effect of the drug. In Neuro Confinement, he had no choice; he had to slow it down. It was like a bad acid trip that never stopped -- things he saw in his mind's eye no one should ever experience -- *Lucy in the Sky with Diamonds. Alligators swimming in the dead of night. Could I watch the eagles fly?* That was what his brain was like; flat out weird, jumping from one thing to another as I often danced the Macarena. Weirdly enough, real, but not.

The funny part was that time inside his mind didn't exist, but the pain was a constant reminder that focused him to either speed up the time or slow it down.

That's the thing, there was real-time, and then there was *mind* time. Trying to explain the difference would be like describing the seven different circles of Hell and how each one was different, yet the same. Rico was in Hell for thirty years, but now he walked among ordinary people with the Devil on his shoulder, who waited, lurked, and watched for an opening for him to fuck up. The moment Rico did, he'd pounce and drive that pitchfork through his chest. Then, he'd belong to the Devil.

Magee finally asked the big question that Rico had dreaded for the past couple of days. "How was it?"

"What do you mean, how was it? How do you think it was? It's more like being dragged by the throat through the gates of Hell by the Devil himself." His mind raced, his thoughts poured out, but no words formed on his tongue. He couldn't even slow his thoughts enough to respond. Nothing spouted forth -- not a single word or mumble. His thoughts spun in a whirlwind of confusion, emptiness, sadness, torment, and desperation. That was until Rico snapped.

He clenched his fists and tightened his jaw. "I'm not going back." He gazed into Magee's eyes and saw her concern as he continued to speak. "I can't do that again! I would rather die than go back to that place in a living Hell."

His thoughts overwhelmed him as his breaths shortened. Beads of sweat formed across his brow. He wanted to cry, but he had no tears left for anything, especially any for himself. I think he emptied his tear ducts during the first year. That meant, he also didn't have any tears left for Magee.

She sensed his torment and despair. "You're fine. I love you." She whimpered before she reached out and hugged him. "Anyway, it's over now. You're back home." Her words to reassure him failed.

Rico's thoughts raced like a rocket blasting into outer space. Her words hit him like a ton of bricks. *I'm back home. My body might be, but I have no soul left. They have taken it.*

Also, without a soul, he realized he couldn't exist. Now he was left in his racing mind wondering what was next. He didn't know the answer. *Do I return home?* Physically, he was only a shell of himself.

At the edge of the platform, Julio stood and stared at his toy truck below. He squatted and leaned, looking down at the track. He glanced to his left -- nothing. He looked to his right -- again, nothing. Instantly, Julio hopped onto the dark and foreboding track three feet below. He paid no attention to his surroundings and had only one mission -- retrieve his toy truck. Stuck in the tracks and securely lodged, Julio fiddled with it. He grabbed it again and pulled as hard as he could, but it still wouldn't budge. Repeatedly, he tugged, pulled, and pushed until the truck finally gave way. The momentum tossed Julio onto his butt. He held up his hand, grasping the truck. "I got it!"

Magee was still in Rico's arms. Neither of them wanted to let go of the other. Their son's words tapped Magee on the shoulder with the subtlety of a two by four. She glanced around the area, searching for him. "Julio?" She waited patiently for an answer. "Julio!" Panic filled her voice as her lips quivered. "Answer me, Julio!"

Magee's demand for Julio to answer met with silence.

Rico's stomach dropped to Hell. He glanced up to look for Julio and couldn't see him either. *Shit!* His mind started into overdrive. *Where is he? Is he in trouble? Had the cigarette guy abducted him? Was he kidnapped? Did he run off? Did a subway creature eat him alive?* His thoughts swirled in his head like a tempest; his mind raced as fast as the blood running through his veins as if he snorted cocaine. Every possible scenario ran through his head.

Rico scanned every inch of the platform for Julio. There was no sign, whatsoever. He took off toward the entrance and bolted up the steps.

A train's whistle echoed through the tunnel as Rico's worst fears took hold taking him where he didn't want to go. His mind became a laser beam, and he could only think of the tracks! *He must be on the tracks.*

His heart pounded; his mind raced back into super overdrive. He ran to the edge of the platform.

Julio popped up, smiling waving his toy truck. The train whistle drifted deafening from around the bend to the platform.

Rico grabbed his ears as his mind played a thousand scenarios of 'What if.' Guilt and horror consumed his unshakable thoughts. *It's my fault that he is in this situation. How could I have abandoned my duty so quickly?*

The train called out to Julio again as he froze in fear. He stared aimlessly at the inevitable.

Rico's mind was with him. *How could I have failed so soon? Only to let my one goodness die while I watch. I must act, but how?*

The train moved fast. Sparks flew as the conductor slammed the brakes.

Rico's mind calculated the possibility of death; It was a high ninety-seven-point two percent that it would occur. That was almost an inevitability, but Rico still grabbed and pulled. A gush of wind tossed him backward, but he had Julio preventing him from getting pulverized. He was safe and unhurt. Rico's heart pounded; his eyes filled with tears of joy. That 'What if,' was too close for his comfort.

Rico let out thirty years of stifled emotions. "My God, what were you thinking?" He screamed at the top of his lungs for a minute, releasing his captive emotions. He pulled him close and cried.

Julio quickly defended his actions. "I needed to get my truck."

Rico's eyes widened. "Are you kidding me? Do you know how close you came to dying?"

Suddenly, a bystander butted in, like this was part of their business. The bystander puffed his chest. "Wow, is he okay?"

Rico ignored the stranger. *It's none of his business.* His mind started racing. *Why is he here? What does he want?* Then his mind switched gears. *I was Julio's protector, and yet I couldn't do that right.* His brain began throbbing again. He moved within three inches of Julio's face. "Do you know what happens when you get hit by a train?"

His thoughts instantly become more focused. Rico had the chance to teach his son a lesson and needed to show him what would happen if he chose to do the wrong things or dangerous things. Rico couldn't bear the thought of losing his son because he was the only pure thing he had left. Fear grabbed him in his throat as Magee rushed over to them.

Rico's mind started to play tricks on him. When he looked at the vending machine, he saw his tortured reflection. His face twitched and slowly became deformed and distorted. *Was that the drug's side effect or is that how I look?*

There he was face-to-face with pure evil. *How can I protect Julio from that monster?* The Devil who sat on his shoulder manifested and split him into two different people -- one who wanted to embrace Julio because he was safe and another who must teach him a lesson to make sure he would never do anything like that again.

Julio stood with fright in his eyes and whimpered.

Rico grabbed him with both hands; his free will at this point now gone. He was a person possessed by the Devil. His eyes seemed to turn red and filled with fire as he spoke to his son. "Do you know what happens when you get hit by a train?"

The whistle of another train snapped his attention, causing him to whip his head toward the train approaching from the opposite direction.

15

Magee sensed a problem with him, and she tried to shield Julio from his wrath. Magee's eyes pleaded toward him. "Rico!"

Julio was unsure what to do as her eyes blistered red from tears.

Rico pulled Julio even closer and gazed into his eyes. "Do you know what happens when you get hit by a train?"

Trembling, Julio finally answered in his meek voice. "No, sir."

The sound of a train became overwhelming. Rico's mind kicked into hyperdrive with raging thoughts. *I must protect him. Keep him safe. Let no harm come to him. Rebuke the Devil.* Suddenly, Rico knew what to do; his path became clear. Even his mind slowed for the first time in thirty grueling years.

As if in slow motion, he looked at the bystander, and wryly smiled. He grabbed him and threw him into the path of the oncoming train.

Splat! Crunch! Blood splattered upward toward them. He turned his attention back to Julio. "That's what happens. You die! Do you understand what I'm telling you? This is what happens when you get hit by a train."

Julio looked petrified as Magee screamed.

"Tell me, Julio, what happens when you get hit by a train."

Julio swallowed as tears erupted like a volcano. "I die."

I am vindicated. The monster on Rico's shoulder disappeared, and he knew that Julio would never do something like that again. His spirits lifted because he had protected his son, and his mind slowed.

Peace fell over Rico as he tightly held a tormented Julio who sobbed in his dad's shoulder.

16

CHAPTER TWO

Meet the Architect

It had been two months since Rico and Julio's subway incident. The company kept the incident a secret from everyone, especially anyone connected to the project. The only reason I knew was that I had linked to him in Neuro Confinement as an observer. I also found a file hidden on my boss' computer. I can be a bit of a hacker sometimes.

My bedroom was well worn. It mirrored my restless mind with piles of books, magazines, and articles which littered the room in a chaotic manner that was controlled, but fighting wanting to get loose. Everything had a place, but you would never think of it as neat and tidy. If anyone moved my stuff, I instantly could tell.

I tried to sleep, but my sweat-drenched body flopped each time hitting the bed as if a rock. It was a marathon session of labored breathing, rapid eye movements, and tossing and turning. I had one explanation why I couldn't sleep -- my nightmares. I'd say they were more like night terrors. Those were the ones that haunt your soul and your very existence. They kept reoccurring night after night with no end in sight. The ones that sooner or later got to me emotionally and made me ask was it all worth the hassle.

I drove on a deserted street inside the perimeter of Interstate 285 in Atlanta, Georgia. It was late at night in a desolate area -- no cars, zero sounds, and no truckers on the old-blacktop country road which snaked around the massively dense scenery.

For a moment, I peered into the rearview mirror and studied the road. It was too quiet, too still for my taste; and I'm the one who likes quiet. I slowly rolled up to the next stop sign. Not sure which way to go, I looked right and then glanced to the left. I looked again. The silence and the emptiness unsettled me. I became a tad paranoid as my eyes roamed searching, right to the left, and back to the rearview mirror over and over. I turned to the left, and for some odd reason, I slowly accelerated.

After I traveled down a slight hill, I spotted a person who stood alone isolated at the stop sign. My car rolled up and came to a stop. As I connected my eyes to the stranger's, he turned away and walked off. *That was strange. I'm not sure what to make of it.*

An uneasiness consumed me. My paranoia consumed me from the tip of my hair to the bottom of my right big toe as I felt an electrical shock radiate down my sciatic nerve. I hastily turned right.

My pace. I must increase my pace. I spotted a fire barrel located at the center of the road surrounded by at least seven vagrants. One man, a hooded figure who loomed taller than the others, slowly turned, sending me into a tremor. *Shit!*

I've been here before, another night, same night terror. Maybe this time I can get it right.

I stopped about a half a block away and cautiously observed. Determined to do something different in my actions to achieve an altered outcome for this nightmare, I tried to change my thoughts. *How many times must I relive this terror?*

The hooded guy turned and took one leap toward me. His eyes seemed as if they belonged to a wolf as he glowered at me. An uneasiness ratcheted throughout my body as I slowly shifted the car into reverse and eased the gas to back into a driveway to turn around. As I put my car into drive, the road filled with a lot more people -- dozens. They all locked onto me with their glowing red eyes. *I am their target.* Oh, shit! I already knew that. *There must be a way to get out of here. Seriously! A Beatle's song.* That was the wrong direction for my schizophrenic nightmare. I didn't know if I was me, myself, or I. *I'll take I.*

Out of nowhere, a thug on a bicycle rode toward my car. I slowed as the guy pulled out a three-foot metal pipe and bashed my car's windshield.

Smack! Crash! Bang!

The glass shattered as I watched the pieces reflect from the moon and in slow motion drifting toward me as if choreographed. *Did I control time and space? That's different. How can something so beautiful be so deadly?*

I covered my face with my arms as the shattered glass hurled toward me like an asteroid, and then they prickled and pierced my skin. It felt as if I poured rubbing alcohol on an open wound when the chards of glass slit my skin. *Wait! Maybe the glass skinned me. I'm already faceless. Now skinless?*

My skin ripped and peeled away. For a moment I thought I saw pieces of my skin float upward and carried off in the breeze. The pain overtook me. I lost control as I swerved my vehicle straight into a parked car. Smash! Clang! Crunch! My head hit the steering column. *Why are the sounds so loud?* Smash, Boom! My head hit the side window. *I think I rolled my car.*

No, a crowd appeared; they rocked my car and chanted in unison. "Die! Die! Die!"

It happened quickly, and I struggled to take a cleansing breath. I was unable to control the environment that my mind created for me. *What the Fuck?* The more I tried, the more chaos and the more voices erupted. Voices! Yes, many voices. Screams! Yes, shrieks! Many, many wailing squawks! *Where is the sound of the subway train when I need it? I learned that from sharing in Rico's Neuro Confinement.*

I focused on a familiar soul-comforting subway train's roar as it barreled toward me in my mind. For a split second, the crashing and smashing stopped only to cease to a deep-black silence only heard in outer space. *Could I possibly control sound too? There was a void in the silence, just like my faceless face. No, I hear my heartbeat.* Thump, thump, wallop, thump! Thwack!

All ages and ethnicities of people filled the streets and surrounded me. Each held unimaginable homemade weapons such as machete ducked taped to a broomstick, a filed downpipe made into a spear, and a crowbar with a spiked ball on a chain that swung from the end. *It takes a sick mind to invent one of those.*

It was easy to tell the inflicted ones from the righteous on a cause. *Really! What's the difference? I challenge you for the answer.* Some were steadfast and vigil while others were ready to purge society of our ills screaming threats of death and disembowelment.

All eyes focused on my morphing Silly Putty flat face as if Picasso painted it. It seemed as if I was a prisoner in a scene right out of a *Frankenstein* movie, and I was waiting for a face transplant. *Maybe Shelly's Frankenstein is real? I didn't think I could be trapped in my mind in Neuro Confinement. Okay, Frankenstein is real. Whose face would I take? Would it be a man's? A Woman's? A child's? What is wrong with me? Oh, yea, Neuro Confinement. This is the end, my friend, the end.*

From that point on, I knew how Jim Morrison felt. *Was this my end? Rider's on the storm, into we're born, rider's in the storm.*

I knew I was losing it; everything I had ever heard since birth now raged war in my mind tormenting me. *Will this ever end?* No, I take that back, they tortured my mind in utter chaos -- all at once, and then tried to Shanghai my soul.

Some sensibility rose within me; I think as I fought off the visions. Still, there was no way out of this tormented terror of a dream.

That's what I missed. It was the drugs; not the Neuro Confinement drugs, the street drugs. *This is the end, my friend, the end. Lost in a wilderness of pain.*

A sharp pain blasted throughout my lower body. I froze in place. I would rather go back to hearing The Doors play and sing *This is the End* than this. Anything, but this! Holy crapfola! Neuro Confinement didn't give you a high. It's the worse low. I missed LSD. Hell, I'd do shrooms. Anything, but this.

21

Wait! There is some semblance of familiarity. Oh, the crowd; it's still here. I tried to breathe, or at least I thought I did. I tried to escape, or at least I thought I did. I tried to make sense of what was happening, or at least I thought I did.

"Die! Torture! Die! Torture! Die!" The crowd harnessed another agenda. They wanted revenge, and the knights were raging war as they stormed toward me. It was the battle of the Knights Templar in my mind -- and they were fighting for King Author, but wait! I was the vagrant and the trespasser. In their eyes, I was pure evil. *Wait! I thought I left this body.*

More and more people filled the street until they merged entirely into a sea of an angry mob.

I grabbed for the door handle and rushed to lock the door, but I was too late as the guy with the steel pipe smashed my side window shattering it into a million pieces toward the sky, and then they drifted like snowflakes to the ground. *I only needed to press one small, little, black button. Whom did I fail? Me? My wife? My children?*

Spit dripped from the right corner of my lip, so I wiped it off, and I swallowed the remainder. Although there was lots of spit in my mouth, my throat and tongue were dry as a dog's bone tossed after a good piece of meat.

My throat closed. I looked around for a weapon; nothing but my fists and my feet.

The no-face guy jerked open my door and snatched me quickly from the car throwing me to the ground. I felt as if a swarm of bees hovered above. I'm deathly allergic to bees, so the outcome terrified me and jolted me further into a frightening horror. My body trembled, my heart raced, and panic gripped my throat.

I tried to fight back, but the more I struggled, the more the mob hit me using clubs, bats, and pipes. Blood flowed from everywhere more, and more people hit me with all types of weapons until my lifeless body couldn't take it anymore.

My astral projection lifted from my body and hovered above them. *Am I dead? Did I die?* A golden cord attached me to my astral-body. I intensely watched as the crowd continued to beat my limp body as they turned into demented demons of myriad shapes, sizes, and colors bent on killing me. I gasped for a large-last-agonal breath as if each dead soul slowly sucked the life from me.

Bam! I bolted awake gasping for air. When I opened my eyes, I was in my bedroom. My gaunt face and haunting eyes looked soulless. Hell, I felt that way too. There was a blackness to them almost as if I had none and as if all the collagen had been sucked away. My face weathered well past my thirties, and I looked as if I turned into a dried prune.

The masking of my nightmares put mileage on me, and my tired body showed it. For a moment, I imagined that my skin peeled from my limbs as I remained faceless. I shook out of that as I leaned forward on the edge of the bed and tried to steady myself. Trying to gather my thoughts, I gazed at the side table where I saw a photograph of my daughter. I studied her face. *I miss her.* It was as if my heart could no longer take the turmoil of her loss. Without a face, my daughter would never find me in the afterlife. That one thought sent trepidation through my spine as if a bullet traveled through it.

Mileage rapidly accumulated on my body. It seemed as my life had been sucked from my carcass. *I can't die this way. Or, should I?*

The clock on the nightstand slowly pounded where each second pulsed like a bass drumbeat in my head. The clock read 3:00 a.m. Some call that the bewitching hour. *Does that mean I can expect witches next in my nightmare? Would they cast the worst spell than the one I'm held into by Neuro Confinement? Shit! My mind won't let me rest. Shit! Shit! Fuck!*

I lumbered to the bathroom feeling the weight of my body as if my bones fractured with every step. The nightmare still haunted me. There was no shaking this one off -- not this time. This episodic ruffian dream was the worse of the three. I felt every pain, heard every nonexistent scream, and tasted my salty blood. Although this dream was always the same, when it came down to it, the variance depended on how far I moved in it and the time for me to recover. Tonight, I traversed almost all the way, but it did stop before the extremely terrifying stuff.

After I shuffled to the bathroom, I felt like I just ran a marathon. I headed directly for the sink, and I leaned on it while I caught my breath. My skin shimmered from the sweat that poured out of my body. I looked like I just got out of the shower wearing all my clothes. Sweat from my pajama bottoms dripped onto the floor which formed a pool at my boney feet.

The roar of my heartbeat, fast, loud, and pounding drowned out my thoughts for a moment, which good because I didn't want to think about it. I tried to move on from it because I discovered after many dreams that this was the best way to handle the terror. I turned on the faucet to splash my face with the chilly water. Sometimes that helped to remove my negative thoughts from the shock of the icy water. I grabbed a washcloth and slowly patted my face dry. Damn! It didn't help this time, but it was a good attempt.

I stared into the mirror, examining my reflection, and wondered why my dreams never changed. *What do they mean? Do I have to wake up before I die in these dreams? If so, how could I have woken up this time? Am I still in the dream state, or did I die?* I saw the gold cord and my astral projection above me. I rose above it all.

The only problem was that it's always the same three dreams night after night. I assumed that if my golden cord was cut, I could not return, and my death would be permanent. *Why was my cord gold? Why was it not silver? Do you have a cord when you die, or does this mean I am not ready to go yet?*

As I pondered these tormented questions, I opened the medicine cabinet and pulled out a bottle of ibuprofen. I guessed eight would be enough this time. I poured them into my hand and closed the mirrored door as a dark shadow roared behind me.

Frightened, I spun around. However, nothing and no one was there. I drew a deep breath to collect my wits, stepped back, and then leaned against the open bathroom door. As I peered at the clock on the nightstand, the number flipped to 3:01 a.m. I can't believe only a minute passed because it seemed like forever. *But, isn't that the point of Neuro Confinement?*

Everything moved in slow motion. It was almost as if I could hear butterfly wings. The dream world now intruded into my real world. The faucet dripped with a thundering sound making me close my eyes lusting for quiet. My eyes popped open, realizing that if I fell asleep again, I would be back in my dream world. *I can't let that happen. I must stay awake.*

I pounded the back of my head on the door in disgust as anguish crept through my soul. It seemed to help with my head pain, and most of all, it kept me awake. I thrust my head backward, hoping for a better result as I clenched my fists watching my knuckles turn white.

I moved my hair out of my eyes while I continued to plunge my head back against the door. Bang! Bang! Bang! Time and again, I thrust my head against the solid surface. I continued to pound until a slow rhythm to my banging developed soothing and curbing my thoughts to take the edge off. The only problem with this strategy was that my head throbbed from the banging. *I am in a no-win situation.* I either banged my head into submission or went insane from the thoughts and the pain.

The eight-ibuprofen waited on me to consume them all at once. Doing so was not the first time, nor would it be the last, but for now it helped although my mind didn't think so. One would think that since it was my mind, I could control it -- not so in Neuro Confinement. That proved to be a battle that I couldn't win.

Morning finally arrived. Mind it; it was a red sky morning reminding me of the old sailor's tale, "Red sky in morning, sailor heed warning," which means storms on the horizon. I entered the kitchen; my hair wild like Albert Einstein's and face unshaven as if a three-day growth took place. The lack of sleep carved deep lines on my face. Although the side-effects dampened my actions, they were methodical intentions. I couldn't help but reflect on my dream. I had analyzed it hundreds, maybe even thousands of times before never homing in on my fears or what they meant which also tormented me.

Nevertheless, I couldn't help but do it again, and for some reason, I stared at the kitchen cabinet as my eyes followed a cockroach making its way into a crack.

Then, I gazed at my feet, realizing that water encroached up to my ankles. I gazed out the window as a massive-foaming wave crashed onto the building with a thundering force. The structure swayed with the tide.

I rushed outside and found myself suddenly on a beach in Grand Isle, Louisiana. The water had flooded the town, and the structures had been inundated. The waves continued to rise. A storm approached as the water at my feet rose quickly. I spotted a sign -- "Mountain View Motel." As I stared at it, something caught my eye. I quickly turned and saw a massive wave a hundred-foot-high coming toward my direction. It towered over me as if I were a spec compared to it.

The lip of the giant wave slowly rolled down as lightning sparked between the rim and the water. The deafening sound surrounded me, and the wave seemed like it was swallowing me whole.

Boom! My bowl hit the countertop.

I grabbed my head as my breathing quickened. My heart thrummed against my ribcage as if it would break it. "Ahh!"

It was another fucking dream. My lack of sleep finally caught up with me. I could fall asleep standing up, even in my kitchen from the fatigue which filled my body.

When I pushed the sides of my head, it helped to stop the pain for a moment. Doing this was how I could get my breathing and pulse to slow. I took a second to collect my thoughts. Then I doused my bowl of cereal with rum and chowed down, knowing it would help somewhat with the pain but could make the lack of sleep worse. I knew this going into my morning meal, but I didn't have a choice.

I entered the living room carrying my bowl of cereal and a black-and-white composition book, and then quickly grabbed the television remote and channel surfed landing on a morning news channel. This helped to distract my mind somewhat, but not as the throbbing overwhelmed any latest information. With my slow sense of time, I developed the ability to multitask. However, the television program showed protesters marching through the streets. I thought about it for a second, then changed the channel to another news channel. A news reporter stood in front of a massive Federal Department of Justice Building as he spoke. "Protests have spread to several distinct parts of the country."

Intrigued, I pushed several books out of my way to sit down. The dining table was the spitting image of mine and was equally crowded with research material as well. Even the chairs were piled high with books. I sat and opened my notebook munching on my cereal as I wrote and watched the news.

The first thing I wrote was -- "Time protocol for the baseline. One minute of mind time was not equal to mind minutes. Therefore, physical time did not equal to mind time. Twenty-four hours equals two years of incarceration. Also, is the military version possibly unstable?"

I circled the word 'unstable' in red, and I wondered what that meant.

Unstable was not truly accurate. While the formula itself was stable, the effects were not. Although getting precise information had been hard to come by, most of what I obtained, I pilfered from the government's or my boss' computers. I even had my backdoor trail to ones the government used. It had been enlightening but still extremely limited. Sometimes it came in dribs and drabs of information that I pieced together. I worked on a solution to this, but it took a while to fix.

I grabbed the remote and flipped the channel to a *Tom and Jerry* cartoon, which made me smile. Then I flicked through more channels stopping to watch the report of a protest. A mob of protesters were hosed down by a military vehicle. That was very depressing and didn't sit well with my cereal.

I continued channel surfing until I landed on a Fox news type program with images of protesters throwing a mailbox through a store window as an O'Reilly type person moderated. "The push to make Neuro Confinement national has prompted overnight rioting outside of the Federal Bureau of Corrections showing the great divide it has caused this nation. Two people deeply involved in this controversy are Senator Bill Candies of Louisiana and Cassandra Reid."

Bill Candies appeared to be charismatic and in his late forties. He flashed a fake-as-they-come grin and waved like most politicians. The only thing missing was him kissing a baby, but I could imagine what that looked like and quickly redirected my thought pattern. I think the baby might have screamed at the top of her lungs if he had tried.

The moderator maintained a cold-fixed stare as he continued to introduce the next spokesperson. "Who is also a medical doctor, and activist Cassandra Reid."

Cassandra was young and bold with her hair fixed in long dreadlocks. She gazed into the camera, almost like a rabbit hit by a bull's eye with no motion or emotion. She seemed more like a mannequin than a human. It was stage fright at its finest.

The moderator cleared his throat. "Look, this is a no brainer. It will save the American taxpayers billions of dollars. What am I missing, Ms. Reid?"

Cassandra pursed her lips before firing off. "Well, it's inhumane for one."

Senator Candies' brow furrowed. "That's ridiculous."

Without missing an opportunity, Cassandra glared toward the senator. "They don't care if they kill prisoners; money is their only motivation."

"Please, when you can't do facts, you attack the messenger."

The moderator adjusted his stance. "Come on, Ms. Reid, that's all speculation at this point. Senator, here's my problem. The public isn't going to buy into shortened prison terms. They're not going to do it. A fifteen-year sentence becomes, what is it?" He shuffled through his notes. "Seven days. To Joe Public, that's a pardon."

"Neuro Confinement is no pardon." Senator Candies slaps his hand onto the podium.

"No! More like government-sponsored brainwashing." Cassandra's belligerent tone irritated the Senator.

Senator Candies wiped his brow. "You make it sound like they're going to become lobotomized or something."

Incensed, Cassandra rolled her eyes. "There are no legitimate long-term studies on this garbage or what it will do to those who undergo the procedure. Are you willing to risk the consequences? What if it were you or a family member? Would you be for Neuro Confinement then?"

When my phone rang, it interrupted the verbal sparring. "Hello?"

"Casey Palmer, please. "The voice on the other end of the line seemed pleasant and not hostile to my relief.

"This is Casey."

The television blared in the background as I tried to focus on the phone call when Cassandra says, "Here's something easy to understand. A former participant, Rico Rodriguez..."

At the mention of that name, I immediately racked my head toward the television with my full attention. I knew that name.

Cassandra took a gulp. "Mr. Rodriquez saved his son from being hit by a subway train."

I focused and turned the volume up.

The voice from the phone continued to invade my focus. "Kevin has to cancel; he'll see you later today."

I ignored the caller and hung up the phone. I then fished out a file, flipped it open, and skimmed it. I needed to find a connection.

"That's a good thing." The moderator's eyes widened.

Cassandra seemed as if fire would shoot from her nose at any second. "Then, to show him what could have happened. He shoved another guy into the path of the oncoming train.

"No! No! No!" Candies seemed as if he foam would drool out from his mouth at any second. Veins popped on his forehead.

Cassandra spat as she spoke. "Then, a week later, he was so distraught that he committed suicide in prison."

I was shocked. I searched the file and identified nothing. *This was how the public first found out about Rico? Did I mention they weren't allowing information about the military formula out? The filthy bastards.*

Senator Candies retorted with a harsh tone ready for battle. "That was already investigated. There was no link to the study."

"We think about twenty percent of the people who take this drug will have some significant psychosis which will range from two months to six years after getting off of it." Cassandra wiped the drool from the corner of her mouth. "Is that a risk you're willing to take, Senator?"

"Where are you getting these figures, Ms. Reid. As a senator, one would think if these were real, I would have access to that information."

"I've directly interviewed over two hundred terrified former inmates. The outcome is dismal for all of them. The facts of the reports don't lie."

I remember reading that final report. It was handwritten and in red across the page were the words -- "No causal connection." I printed the name, Cassandra Reid on a scrap piece of paper, I added a question mark and circled it in red. I needed to discover who she was and what she knew about Neuro Confinement. It seemed as if she knew more than I did, and I invented it. No telling which, but I intended to find out, and she was my only lead. *Which version of the drug are they using? Mine or the military's.*

Senator Candies stepped up to defend the program. "Recidivism is high, and this must change. What we know is that seventy-seven percent of current inmates get rearrested within five years. No sooner than they are released, they are back on the street, and they commit another crime, are rearrested and imprisoned, costing taxpayer's hard-earned income. The bleeding must stop, and Neuro Confinement is the only way to address this crisis. With Neuro Confinement, the recidivism rate has plummeted, and ninety-two percent of prisoners become fully rehabilitated. In a follow-up study performed by an independent firm, former inmates reported that they have no desire to commit any crime that would put them back into the system. They fear Neuro Confinement, not a prison. Their fear leads them to become productive members of our society."

She tilted her nose high in confidence. "That's because they're scared to death to be put on that drug again."

A smug grin contorted on Senator Candies' lips. "Tell me how that's not a win for society?

"That one is simple. Former prisoners live in constant fear of night terrors that drove them mad. They become so distraught that they become dysfunctional. If they are dysfunctional, society will pay out the nose to house them, clothe them and feed them."

Night terrors? That was the term I knew best because they haunted me and eroded my brain night after night. *What did I create?*

I moved closer to the television and stared at Ms. Reid, wanting to know what she thought. To learn what she knew, I tried to read her mind and quickly concluded that she might be the one that could piece this all together for me.

CHAPTER THREE

The Belly of The Beast

This was the belly of the beast so to speak. I am not sure how I feel about Clayborn BioMedical. Some said it reminded them of prison with its large sprawling modern layout. To me, the interior corridors were wide, bright, and the sunlight popped in from various windows giving it a dichotomy of Heaven. However, many swear that the secure high-tech features reminded them that it could be Hell. I usually let them make up their minds. Remember, dealing with matters of the brain was where I excelled?

I stood in a corridor which led to an area called, "The Nursery." Whenever we entered any room, we needed to put on a lab coat to maintain a sterile environment. I grabbed one off the rack right before we entered the multiple person treatment room, which was one of my favorite spots in the whole place. It was my baby, and it took almost ten years of my life to get it to this point. I kept the room dimly lit to avoid any unwanted or unnecessary stimuli to the patients. Many of the staff reported that it reminded them of a nursery at bedtime, hence the name.

The tubes and wires that coursed along the bodies of a dozen prisoners reminded those that these were no babies as most were serving a ten to thirty-year confinement for their various crimes and categorized as evil white-collar criminals. I had come to understand that you never knew what evil was in those criminals' hearts because once pushed, their true nature surfaced like it or not.

One of the coolest things was that the Neuro Confinement prisoners appeared to float in mid-air on contoured stainless-steel pedestal beds. That was a design I took pride in because it took a year of planning. The tables looked cold and uncomfortable. However, it gave the illusion of weightlessness, and each one covered with lambskin padding served a purpose. The contoured body shape of the table was honestly extraordinarily comfortable and stopped the need for repositioning a convict during a session. Those sessions could last up to thirty days, so I chose stainless steel because of the non-corrosive aspects after many failures with other materials. We had problems with pathogens on some earlier designs and experiments, the last change to stainless steel, resulted in no issues.

The criminals stayed in one position for the entire time so that no additional stimuli mingled into the mix, which proved to be a massive problem during changing time. Families became quite upset when the subjects were kept an extra week in Neuro Confinement when they were accidentally brought out of a session by a movement or additional stimuli which interrupted their treatment. Trust me; it wasn't pretty to watch.

The Neuro Link was the brainchild of Kevin's, although I have performed many tweaks to it by adding a stainless-steel ring that adorned each inmates' head. Cold blue lasers mounted on the rings on the sides of their skulls popped on and illuminated the lab with a bright teal-blue hue. People think the color gave a sense of coldness, but the patients never saw it, so I guess it was an acceptable modification. The trick was to get into the brain, quickly without causing trauma. We tried everything to the point we did experiments where we inserted needles into different lobes of the brain. The result proved that germs were always a significant issue with this improvisation.

Kevin stumbled upon the work of Fredrick Germane who discovered how to get images inside the brain via lasers. Kevin modified it for our needs. Lately, I have pushed it further to the limits, but I'll get to that later. I noticed a clock on the wall, which read 11:30 a.m.

Oh shit, I'm late; let's go. This is the shortcut to the consultation rooms.

The room looked like a typical doctor's examination room with stark white painted walls, an exam table, and a sink. I sat on a small round doctor's stool and examined papers on my clipboard.

Tyler, thirty-year-old with a crew cut, square jaw, and former military, sat patiently across from me as I read his chart. One of my bad habits was rolling my ink pen between my fingers. Some found it annoying, especially when I tapped it like a drumstick.

Tyler bit his lower lip. "I didn't do what they said I did."

I paused and flashed a whatever-smile. I have had so many criminals plead their innocence that I found it laughable, and I concluded it was a type of defense mechanism. Each of the criminals desired to be recognized as the good guys even though they had fucked up. I held my laughter to the inside before I spoke. "At this point, it doesn't matter what you think or your guilt or your proclaimed innocence, does it?"

"I know, but I just wanted you to understand. I don't steal things. I have morals." Tyler's lips formed a weird smile as beads of sweat formed across his upper lip.

I smiled back, trying to acknowledge his fear. "Okay. I understand, but I have a job to perform. Your proclamation of innocence doesn't change the outcome; now does it?"

Tyler heaved a gut-wrenching sigh. "Really? I'm just ready to get this over with, so I can get back to my family. I've been an absentee father, three tours in the sandbox, now this. I haven't seen my boy in almost a year."

I smiled inwardly. I think I liked Tyler in some strange way. He seemed sincere, and for a moment, I felt sorry for him. Not because he was a criminal, but that he had to be away from his son. I would have given anything to have more time with my daughter. "When are you scheduled for Neuro Confinement?"

"The twenty-fifth at eight."

I wrote Tyler's time and date in my notebook and circled it.

Tyler shivered like a child. "Is this going to hurt?"

The pain from undergoing Neuro Confinement was one of the biggest fears of the prisoners. *They should have thought of that before committing a crime.* "Not at all. Just focus on a flaw. Are you religious?"

Tyler reflected for a second as his eyes darted upward, and then he flashed a strange-little smirk. "Somewhat, why? Is it important?"

"Not really, but many people say they see God and talk to him. It changed their lives for the better." I looked at my pen. It rested about two inches from my fingers; and oddly, it rolled toward my hand. I picked it up and completed several more mandatory forms.

Tyler looked at me almost with a smile. "Thanks for caring; few people would take the time to be nice and try to put people at ease about what to expect. I'm scared to death."

"Yeah, sure." I'm not certain if Tyler heard the sarcasm in my voice. *Again, don't do the crime if you don't want to suffer the consequences.* I looked at my watch and quickly gathered my things. I was late, like always, which became like an ongoing joke in the lab.

My colleagues always mocked me. "If you want Casey on time, lie to him. If you want him there at noon, tell him eleven-thirty."

At least I was consistent in my behavior by being always late by twenty-five minutes.

The Neuro Confinement candidates, as I called them, had the same worries. Would it hurt? For me, I questioned if I would discover what transpired during their crime? They all wanted to know if I could read their minds. Now that was interesting to me. According to what was in the literature, there was no way to access people's thoughts or to experience their feelings. However, I knew better because not only could I hear their deepest and most secret thoughts but also, I experienced them in some shape or fashion. It was as if I absorbed their hopes, fears, and yes, their nightmares once inside Neuro Confinement. I found their nightmares extremely disturbing for the most part. Although now and then I was surprised by the depth of their guilt or sometimes the lack of it which terrified me more. For those who failed to show remorse or empathy, I knew they were psychopaths and deserved Neuro Confinement.

Have you ever met someone without a soul? I did. Those were the most disturbing ones of all because they derived pleasure from what would cause you or me to hurl. So, imagine this, you think someone's thoughts, and they were ready to do something evil that you would never do, but they go through with it and revel in it. Your body reacts in unexpected ways with feelings of joy or possibly an erection while being disgusted out of your mind. I worried that it could turn me into a schizophrenic. I probably needed therapy after these mind visits. I am not certain why I didn't other than I was the doctor and not the patient.

CHAPTER FOUR

Numbing My Pain

I spent tcn years developing my Neuro Confinement drug. Developing this drug took me on a path that few have ventured. To completely understand this medication, you would have to comprehend my starting point.

About twelve years ago, I lost Julie, my daughter. She was my life and the joy of my heart. After her death, I just wanted to escape from everything. It was a known fact that tragedies either tore families apart or brought them closer together -- this one, without a shadow of a doubt, shredded mine into fragments of despair. Honestly, I adjusted to my daughter's death better than my wife, Roxanne.

Our heartbreak was too much for Roxanne to take, and she drew deep within herself and separated herself from me. I missed Roxanne the moment she left me. She was such an incredible person. We separated less than a year after that night. I thought about her often, and I hadn't seen her in years when I saw her from a distance a few months ago. Seeing her again stopped me in my tracks. I decided to turn around and left instead of running into her -- more about that later.

Anyway, I searched for ways to zone out. I tried lots of standard methods. The first one was boozing. It began as a drink or two a night but quickly became a fifth every two days. By drinking a little more each day, I never realized how much I drank until it was way too late.

My drink of choice was twenty-one-year-old Scotch, Glenfiddich to be exact -- a single malt that was one of the last independently brewed scotches in Scotland. I always loved a great scotch with a fine cigar. The problem with scotch was that it tended to burn a hole in my stomach, which only took a year at the rate I drank.

Finding yourself in the emergency room, throwing up blood was not a fun experience. They said it was stress related. Imagine that; I was stressed out to the gills by my daughter's death and my wife leaving me. What did I have to be stressed over?

After the hospital visit, I decided I would take time off to travel and see the world. The only thing that didn't change was my need to escape. So, I sought different methods to numb my pain. I wanted to get lost, but with a purpose to zone out.

I decided to take a weekend getaway to Amsterdam. It was my first trip out of the country. I remembered flying into Amsterdam during a snowstorm. It was mid-April, and I couldn't believe it snowed this late in the year. I also realized that I failed to pack warm clothes. After a trip to Hema, the Target of Amsterdam, I finally warmed. I booked a room at the Botel, a boat converted into a hotel and permanently docked in one of the canals. I thought it would be cool to stay somewhere different for a change.

That first night I decided to hit the local coffee shop to find weed to take the edge off my travels. To call the place a coffee shop did not give it justice. When you think of coffee shops, most people thought of a Starbucks or the typical American hipsters' hangout like the Lucky Bean. The place I picked was more like a modern block party night club with open fire pits, DJ's, and hundreds of partiers. The music was very European techno and not my type, but it made everything feel like an exciting combination.

Inside the coffee shop, except for a couple of tourists inside who were there for hedonistic purposes, local twenty-somethings who knew how to party inhabited the place. Everything about them said let's party in their attitudes and behaviors.

One of the things I learned was that Amsterdam didn't like its reputation as a Magical Drug Wonderland. They wanted to attract older wealthier tourists from Russia and China and not people like me who were there for the guilty pleasures of sex, drugs, and rock-n-roll.

The first night I made my first mistake, and I started with the local stout beer. Later in the night, I switched to pot. The beer and the pot together, wow, it was just enough to make me puke. At this point, I was a rookie and had smoked a little skunk back in college; but nothing like this new shit. So, unless you have uncovered a hangover cure, please don't do it.

The next night I started with "Space Cakes." Space Cakes were a local pot-infused edible. They were quite tasty, but being a novice, I thought I could handle it. Boy, I was wrong. I later learned how to pace myself, but those first few nights I was not quite sure how I got back to my botel. It did cost me about two hundred in cash that I had on me that night. I was aggressive with my dose once I had them. I remembered calling them "Baby Cakes." It even became my nickname for a few days. All sorts of crazy shit filled those nights, and most of which I couldn't fully remember as they emerged as faded images. The drug scene in Amsterdam became old fast. I had gone there looking for an escape; and not a way of life. I mean, how could I dare party with my baby girl in the cold hard ground?

One of the things I learned was that if I jumped on the Eurorail at the precise time that the train was to leave, they were always on time, and I would be on the right train for free. This time I was headed to Paris, or so I thought I mean it had worked for a week. What could go wrong? Anyway, I made my way through the train looking for a seat. The train was full, so I sat in a nearly full car. I looked at my watch; it was 9:30. I struck up a conversation with a twenty-something German woman who sat next to me closing me in at the window.

It was an exciting conversation until I suddenly realized that we had not made two scheduled stops. I eased my lips next to her ear. My breath fanned her neck. "Where are you heading to?"

She recoiled quickly. "Barcelona."

Oh, shit! This isn't good. I sunk into my seat and scarfed down several more Space Cakes.

We began to fall asleep after we exhausted ourselves from chatting around midnight. Unfortunately, my stomach wasn't ready to go to bed. I felt the familiar pangs of nausea as I fruitlessly tried to go to sleep. I

43

knew those cheese sandwiches wanted out -- big time. Around three a.m., they were finally hurled out. Not wanting to stop the train and disturb everyone much less disturb my seatmate while I yakked, I ripped my sweatshirt off and threw up into it.

I tied it up into a little ball and put it neatly beneath my seat. Crisis averted! When we stopped at a rest stop an hour later, I was able to wash my shirt in the sink. My friend Carey looked at me strangely as if to wonder why on earth I was doing laundry in a sink at 4:00 a.m., but I managed to avoid the issue with a cockamamie excuse about needing to get rid of a stain.

The next morning, we finally arrived in Amsterdam. My first stop on the agenda was to locate a coffee shop -- which in this country was a bar.

The Grasshopper was a dark, dank bar. Every other bar in Amsterdam oozed with the smell of grass, weed, skunk, or whatever. What seemed seedy in any other country was perfectly reasonable in Amsterdam. Can you believe that? The coffee shops attracted a random, eclectic crowd from dirty hippies and derelict potheads to Euro-trash and frat boys. Everyone desired a toke; even me,

My friend Tina and I decided to go for gold and ingested several Spaced Out Cakes. FYI, this was nothing like pot brownies. Spaced Out Cakes consisted of hash with a bit of cake mixture into it. They warned me to be careful about eating them, but without a doubt, I had to eat one more before I left. Wouldn't you? I ate cheese in France, didn't I? I drank beer in England! It was my duty as an excellent traveler to savor the most exquisite Dutch delicacies; so, I did.

We decided to purchase one pan of Spaced Out Cakes and split it three ways. As I swallowed my first bite, I tasted the hash. After an hour, I felt a little funny as if the walls closed in on me like those seen in a Looney Tunes cartoon when Bugs Bunny tried to escape the room. I freaked and decided I needed to get the hell out of this place.

After the Baby Cakes, I indulged in another local delicacy called truffles -- not the ganache filled chocolate delicacy. These were more like magic mushrooms. One night after I took one, I thought I could fly and wound up with paramedics rescuing me out of one of the canals. The cops were not amused. I guess I thought I was Superman and I'm glad I didn't try to beat a speeding bullet or a speeding locomotive.

After being in Amsterdam for about a month, I felt like I was wasting my life and realized nothing changed except I ran with the dregs of society. I began to harbor a dislike and distrust I had never known. I remembered one morning waking up in a heroin den and knew I had hit rock bottom. The smell and the sights reminded me of death.

I couldn't take it any longer. I loathed living like the person that took Julie away, which disgusted me. In essence, I became him in a way or at least my version of him. I thought I was right and just, but I was trying to escape reality, and my demons that filled my nightmares night after night won. I remembered passing a newsstand seeing an article about the USA, and then something snapped in my brain. I was ready to return home, and I needed to get my life together. So, I got on the next flight headed back to the States. The flight home was arduously long.

After a couple of months back home, I became wanderlust again. By this time, I wanted to move my life forward, so I took up meditation. I tried to find a purpose; that's when I made the decision that changed my life forever. An instructor named Sherman led my meditation class. We talked a lot, and believe it or not, he was a Shaman from a small Peruvian tribe in the Andes -- Sherman, the Shaman; what a name. It still makes me smile to this day, but it almost had an unfortunate ring to it. He planned a trip back home, so I worked my way into being invited.

We traveled from New York to Lima. That was the easy part. After we landed, it began to look like a journey straight out of *National Geographic*. To get to his village, we started with a four-day river journey. I was excited to see the scenery. We started on the Amazon River in a small traditional bright blue Indian wooden boat in necd of a serious paint job with a straw-covered roof. The motor was like a Go Devil made for operating in shallow waters.

One of the things I remembered the most was how fast the river ran. I had been on the Mississippi River, and the current was treacherous. The current looked like it stood still, but if anything went into the water, it was immediately swept downstream at an alarming speed. Four days on the boat cured me of seeking my adventure. I just wanted a hot shower and a warm bed. I needed a good night's sleep.

The sights amazed me; however, we traveled very deep into the rainforest in which I spent four days without hearing anyone speak other than our crew. The trip was still fantastic.

The picture in my head was so far off from reality that it wasn't funny. I pictured it like a missionary meeting an uncivilized tribe in the Amazon. When I first lay eyes on Sherman's village, it devastated me. The place looked like a rundown primitive fishing village although modern society made its footprint on this place. The area was like a shanty town with electricity and a few light poles, but several of the dwellings didn't have four walls. The older villagers wore tennis shoes and Western t-shirts. The kids wore shorts and didn't have shoes or shirts. Some houses were on stilts off the ground anywhere from six to eight feet. I assumed it was because of the rising river waters, floods, or typhoons. Everywhere I looked, it made me depressed. Kids played about, although they felt deep pangs of hunger because there wasn't enough food for the villagers. I understood why Sherman left this place, although his heart never did.

As we walked down the street, people began to pour out of their doorways. Nothing ever changed, so when a newcomer arrived, there was a buzz in the community. After someone recognized Sherman, they greeted both of us like royalty. Curious, the kids came around to get a look at the Westerner. I admitted that I enjoyed the moment. However, I became self-conscious for the first time in my life. I was now in the minority.

When the elders learned that we had arrived, they ordered a feast. I was embarrassed that they thought of spending what little they had on me. It made me feel guilty. The town took me in as one of their own, and I stayed with them for about a month.

Sherman wanted to teach me some of his ways. I was looking for the next high. That caused a significant oxymoron in my life. We sat to talk. Sherman stared into my soul. "Every heard of ayahuasca?"

"I have not."

"Ayahuasca is a hallucinogenic medicinal plant used by an indigenous Shaman of central America."

"Let's do it!"

"If only you are ready to change your life, I'll introduce you our local medicine man who is also a Shaman. He's a student of mine."

"That sounds incredible."

"He takes over for me when I leave the village. Are you interested?"

"Indeed. Like I said, let's do it."

"It will make you deal with your daughter's death."

This hits me hard. *Am I ready for this?*

"To receive healing from her death, you must go through a cleansing ritual, taking ayahuasca."

"That can't be that bad, can it?"

"There is an upside to taking Ayahuasca and a downside. A few people die from ayahuasca every year."

"What?"

"They sought to be enlightened, but sometimes the Shaman didn't administer the drug as they should, or they were inept. You must be careful and take your time in your cleansing to do it right. For me, I roamed the jungle for seven years before becoming a Shaman. You must not be in a hurry."

"Are you telling me it could take seven years? Wouldn't it be easier just to purchase ayahuasca off the streets?"

"The ayahuasca tourism boom was a blessing and a curse to our village. It brought the Western world to our doorstep, and the impact was not positive. It enslaved some of us and stole what little we possessed. Sometimes, growth is positive, but not always."

His words to me almost sounded like he prepared and mastered the same speech. "I'm sorry about that. That does seem to put a damper on things. It's hard to tell whom to trust nowadays."

"You are so correct in believing that because there are local sorcerers who call themselves Brujos. They masquerade as a Shaman to steal other's mojo and energy. Every human only has a certain amount of personal energy which can be used during one's lifespan. Again, you must be careful on your journey. You must have someone to guide you and act as your watcher."

"I trust you to be there for me. Will you guide me?"

"I will direct your journey. One of your goals is to develop your intuition and use it along with patience."

"I'm not sure if I'm following you."

"You will, when you bond with your spirit guide in the jungle. It is something that you will have to learn for yourself. It will come to you gradually and naturally."

"How so?"

"When your journey begins, I'll give you the tools you'll need in your dream world. It will be there that you must dig down within yourself for the answer. I cannot help you in that area."

We prepared several days before my cleansing ritual began. Several days before it was planned to start, Sherman took me into the jungle to forage for what I needed. Every step seemed planned out. It started with a diet of mushrooms, tree bark, and a few plants. *Was this a ritual in and of itself?*

He spent time teaching me about the medicinal plants and showed me how to survive by my hand and using what was in front of me. We sat to discuss my next lesson on ayahuasca.

Sherman held up a plant. "You must purge your system first, so the ayahuasca has the freedom to control your spirit."

Those are the words I remembered the most as they became one of the founding blocks of my early research.

"You must completely devote yourself to the ancient wisdom passed to me by my ancestors that I pass onto you." Sherman's eyes pierced my soul as I listened.

It all seemed like mumbo jumbo to me at first. I was getting angry and wanted desperately to get on with my journey. Finally, the day came for us to pick the fresh ayahuasca, but that didn't happen without an elaborate ritual.

"You must pray to the ancestors before the cutting for guidance."

I'm not sure praying to my ancestors was necessary before but deciding on which part of the plant to cut was fascinating and made me a believer by observing Sherman's faith, dedication, and teachings.

I learned that ayahuasca had two essential ingredients, plus a few kickers depending on the intent of the person who took it. One part was the brew of a plant called Banisteriopsis Cappi or a Monoamine oxidase inhibitor (also called MAO inhibitors or MAOIs) to treat depression and panic disorders that defined the neural inhibitor. Most Shamans considered this drug to be the spirit of the ayahuasca. It's a bright green tropical vine with pink flowers that grew to about ninety feet and twined its way onto other trees and plants for support. Thank goodness for the vibrant pink flowers because they made the plant easier to identify.

Sherman glared at me with his brow furrowed. "Only pick the vines with the pink flowers because those are more appropriate for you. You're lucky; the vine just bloomed in January because it is ready to give."

"They can feel your loss and your pain. It's almost overwhelming the amount of information to know."

"Also, you must thank each vine for giving before you take what you want. This thinking also permeates several cultures, such as American Indian, Buddhism, and even Hindu."

"Are you serious?"

Sherman placed his knife close to a vine. "Thank you for your glorious flowers. May my ancestors watch over me and our future visions."

"So, I have to pray to a vine?"

"Stay to form. Do not stray your life can depend on it."

I stayed with his thoughts, and before I cut the vine, I took a deep breath and prayed in a somewhat sarcastic manner. "Thank you vine for your flower and thank Sherman's ancestors for watching over us and our future visions." I glanced up at Sherman as I held onto the vine. "Happy now?" The vine dropped down on his head. It was like the vine was trying to teach me a lesson.

"Yea, I'm happy now. I am not the one who needs to find happiness." He couldn't help but laugh out loud. "Allow the flowers to work in you at the right time. You're an asshole sometimes. It's for your own good."

We continued to cut the flower vines, and we thanked each vine and his ancestors for our future visions.

The other part was the N-Dimethyltryptamine (DMT or *N*-DMT) containing plant called Psychotria Viridis, which altered time and reality and caused those who took it to hallucinate. Although Sherman told me that he swapped other forms of DMT plants, he always added some of this plant in the brew he made based on his spirit guides' recommendation. The DMT plant was another bright green plant that looked like a large bush with small reddish-brown berries. However, the ones Sherman instructed me to pick had green nubs more like a plant that hadn't matured yet. It's like a rattlesnake bite was enough to kill you; size isn't always important.

We talked about everything under the sun during the day picking the vines. That was when he homed in on Julie. Pain gripped me deep within. "How did you know about Julie? I had no idea you knew because I didn't talk about her anyone."

"I have the gift of a Shaman who can pinpoint your pain." He clipped another vine. "Thank you for your beauty. Thank you, my honored ancestors, for leading us in our future vision."

His words haunted me as I clipped my next vine.

"You didn't thank the vine. That is not good. You must always thank the vine."

At that moment, the vine seemed to come alive. It felt like an LSD, but only for a fraction of a second. I was taken back as Sherman smiled. He felt what I saw. This time I spoke to the vine with conviction. "Thank you, vine. Thank you, Sherman's ancestors. Thank you for our future visions."

"My ancestors are pleased. They told me to bring you into a deeper spiritual journey. This is something you need and must do."

Sherman used various herbs to make the ancestor-led concoction.

"What goes into this concoction?" I waited for the answer.

"I will share with you at the right time. Patience must develop deep within."

I never was a patient man, but he eventually changed me. That formula was the part of the concoction I continued to use in my daily practice. The only problem -- he failed to teach me how to determine what a person needs.

I'm glad Sherman called it a healing ritual because, after the first session, I thought he tried to kill me. Then again, he may have wanted me to freak out and vomit a lot. It seemed like the medicine man enjoyed watching me go through the pain.

"You must embrace old traditions, remember the vine."

"Old traditions my ass." I think it was part of a cottage industry filled with pomp and circumstance that didn't make much sense aimed to get Westerner's money. However, because of my vine vision, I surrendered to my journey. I trusted Sherman's judgment on this Shaman, and for some odd reason, I felt he had my back as peace overcame me.

After that first session, the tribal medicine man gave me a heart-to-heart talk.

"You have a complicated illness; your spirit guides assured me you'll get through this. Rest assured, I have Sherman's impeccable work ethic that will get you through. There is one more thing I must inform you as your protector. I won't treat you unless you are ready."

The day of the big ritual was upon us. I remembered the dreary and overcast weather because I wanted it to be unique. We built a fire in the clearing of the jungle. The greenery was amazing as I gawked at the sight in front of me as the vines became alive. Both my body and mind immediately traveled to the fourth dimension. All of this time, Stephen Hawking had gotten it right. There are multiple dimensions. I was alone but amazed as I stood within a cubed area below the surface of a water barrier. When I looked up, I saw the forest and the bright green vines with pink flowers. They were happy if that makes sense. They seemed to wave at me. An ancient withered man pushed through the vines toward the barrier and passed through it. "Grandfather?"

"Your grandfather's spirit lives within you. He is here to guide you through your journey."

My grandfather morphed into a humanlike plant blending in with the rest. "Calm your mind and spirit son. It would be best if you accepted what comes forth. Don't let it control you, but you control it. Do you understand?"

"Not exactly. I don't know how to control my journey."

A purple and shimmering vortex formed and sucked me into it. I became a plant too and felt everything they felt and heard everything they said during that first ayahuasca experience. I connected to the spirit of my grandfather and talked with the spirit of plants too. Ayahuasca was now a vital part of me.

The plant can be hazardous. Some travelers misunderstood the health benefits of this medicine. There were also foreigners who used ayahuasca as an exciting way of getting high or fucked up. The danger of that was if you weren't prepared, if you didn't follow the diet, and if you didn't know what you were doing, you couldn't benefit from taking it. That was why many people ended up having bad experiences too. The drug did more harm than good when digested for the wrong reasons, and a person's body had not been cleansed. Think of it as a bad LSD trip on steroids.

There's a widespread misunderstanding among many people that ayahuasca wasn't a drug, but they were wrong. It fixed and relieved so many illnesses which proved the healing power. That said, the drug wasn't a quick fix either, and I used it in a slow, gradual, and deliberate process. Most people took ayahuasca dozens of times over an extended period to heal. However, many didn't have the patience for that and would go on a holiday and received futile results. Patience was the very core of ayahuasca.

Westerners realized there was money to be made from it and quickly industrialized the plant establishing Western-run retreat centers like illegal mining. They came to steal the ancient wisdom and sold it for profit.

When I first started, ayahuasca was all about healing people. It used to be about diagnosing illness to help people to improve. Not anymore. Companies were commercializing this plant and ultimately contaminating the culture of ayahuasca.

Even worse, there were Shaman training programs. People came, signed up to a course, took a few workshops, maybe received certification, and then called themselves a Shaman treating people who proved extremely dangerous. Come on. Even I knew that someone couldn't become a Shaman in two weeks. It would be like a doctor operated on someone after two weeks of training and not having the proper equipment.

Sherman was adamant to whom he treated. For example, he would only treat people with severe physical ailments and refrained from treating people who came to seek an adventure. Although my Shaman and Sherman never taught me how to identify those type of clients, I easily distinguished between those individuals with ease and confidence. When I consulted the plants as one, they isolated for me those clients who needed ayahuasca and who didn't. The plants never lied. This ran contrary to the for-profit Shaman culture.

Ayahuasca activated the part of the brain called the amygdala, which stores our emotional memories. Several people died from participating in these rituals or became psychotic. I quickly learned that one must face yourself, which was one of the most frightening things a person could do. *The storm is coming.*

At the first ceremony, the paranoia overwhelmed me. I didn't expect that. Once I stopped resisting, things improved. I went through lots of negative and positive emotions. Insecurities emerged, and emotions like sadness took over. When I connected to my higher self, I discovered what made me happy, although my ego held onto my traumas not wanting to let go.

The second ceremony was one I would never forget and by far was the most intense experience of my life shaking me to my core, which made me go through my worst fear -- a living nightmare. Visually my senses were overwhelmed, and my tactile sensations, hearing, and seeing colors became enhanced. I tasted my thoughts, which proved intensely weird stuff. I experienced a panic attack quickly descending into my inner madness.

I started questioning reality. *What is time? Is there a God? Do I belong? Is this real? Am I real? Is the earth real? Do I live in a matrix?* My turmoil and the inner battle intensified to a boil.

My deepest fears soon surfaced as I experienced anguish, terror, anger, and rage. I accepted that these were my primal negative emotions. I went into a timeless dimension which resembled a black void. It was indescribable super intense. I convinced myself that I would be stuck in this psychotic episode forever. I purged a great deal as I cried and asked for it to end. The spirits didn't hear my screams and failed to recognize my pain and turmoil.

I hurled vomit, which was more than my body emptying my stomach and detoxing. Instead, it was my boding purging myself of my emotions, feelings -- lust, hate, fear, and everything else negative in my life I'd held onto for my entire life. I got to the point where I thought my only way out was to end my life. At the time, I thought there was no other option other than suicide.

The Shaman shoved a bit of lime and salt into my mouth. Very quickly, I crashed back into my reality. I wasn't fighting with the spirits; I was struggling with myself in a heated and unconquerable battle. I was a tad nervous, jumping back into the next ceremony, which was very scary, but I had no choice. The purple and silver vortex swallowed me into blackness. Nothing happened. I now thought it was all a waste of time.

However, the last ceremony, I received all the answers I needed. Finally, my spirit guide gifted me with the knowledge I sought. I had to escape to that place where I was utterly alone to face my biggest darkest fears -- deep fears, desires. It all made sense to me now. It was an awesome place -- clean, light, vibrant, and rejuvenating, allowing me to shed all the cultured programming like snakeskin peeling away from me. I accepted that as a person I needed to fall in love with the shadows of my life and own them rather than push them to the deepest recess of my subconscious.

CHAPTER FIVE

The Nature of The Problem

It was bumper to bumper traffic, which was one of the things I detested most about working in a big city. It's not only the crowds and pollution but also the general disregard of humans toward their fellow man. I looked up and saw the Federal Justice Department building. I was just about there when I glanced at my watch -- seven minutes after ten. I slammed my fist against the steering wheel because I recognized that I screwed up. They always told me half an hour earlier than I needed to be there, but now I'm an hour late.

As I inched closer to the building, a car pulled out of a parking spot two parking spaces in front of me. It looked like the parking fairies were with me as I had received a little luck after all. *Those that don't look up front don't park upfront.* I pulled into the favored spot and raced for the exit.

I dashed toward the building as I glanced at my watch again. Time always fucked with me. When I needed it to slow down, it sped up and vice versa. I entered the Federal Justice Department foyer that gave off a cold and impressionable vibe which could send shivers down an average person's spine. I showed my identification badge and placed my belongings into a plastic tray next to an x-ray machine. I passed through it, and Dr. Kevin Winfield, thirty-years-old and devilishly handsome, met me. He always wore an Armani suit and looked very put together, and that day was no variance. I eyed my watch.

Kevin approached me. "Are you ever on time? Did you have another rough night? You look like it."

My face hardened. "You're a dick. Let's get this over with."

"I was just trying to be sincere, have you slept since the lab?"

"Does it look like it?" He knew better than even to ask me that question. How dare he go there after all that I've done for him when he needed my help?

I remembered the time when he became so drunk he nearly got us kicked out of the Ritz Carlton in New Orleans. Bourbon Street was always a fun time, but sometimes Kevin couldn't hold his liquor, and this time was no exception. He insisted he was a dog and during the night he crawled on his hands and knees back to the hotel. Kevin was so wasted that he went into the revolving door and kept going in a circle. I think he was chasing his tail. Now, remember he was on his hands and knees pushing the door round and round. The spinning caused him to get sick, and he hurled in the entrance. If that wasn't enough, he passed out, which made the door unable to turn.

The hotel management wasn't pleased and would have kicked us out until yours truly stepped up to the plate and smoothed things over with the manager, which cost me a couple of hundred dollars. Anyway, I just wanted to provide you a taste of our relationship.

***

An officer opened the door, and we headed into another long hallway.

Our boss, Marcus Lynch, gray, mid-fifties, with an overbearing Napoleon complex, waited nervously around the corner as we approached. Lynch's eyes widened as he stepped toward us. "They're having second thoughts and are talking about stopping the nationalization of the program. Senator Candies is pissed. He found out about the lab yesterday."

Kevin and I knew this meant it wouldn't be a cakewalk during the hearing.

"Can we keep the funding without going national?"

Lynch quickened his step ignoring the question.

We continued down the corridor. I poked Lynch on his shoulder to get his attention. "Hey, can we keep the funding without going national?"

Lynch shook his head. "No way. If they take it off the ballot, we're screwed, and our stock prices will tank. A hit like that would be unrecoverable. We can't let it happen."

I understood what that meant. "Is that why you started putting violent offenders into the program -- stock prices?"

Lynch remained silent. He knew better than to confront me here. To say he was a worm would be an understatement. However, sometimes, you must dance with the Devil if you sold your soul to get a project made. He knew I didn't give a rat's ass about the price of their stock, and I sometimes pushed the limit further than I should.

We made it to the entrance to the hearing. An officer approached us. "They've been waiting on you."

Kevin straightened my tie. "You ready, honey?"

I gave him a not-right-now glower. He backed off as the officer opened the door to the chambers. I cleared my throat. "We'll see."

Lynch moved closer to my ear. "Remember, nothing about violent offenders. Don't say anything that can come back and bite you or us in the ass. I'm warning you."

I stopped and turned to Lynch. "Unlike some people, I have nothing to hide. I'm an open book."

Lynch's jaw tightened as he huffed. "Just don't do it. This is my last and final warning."

I sloughed him off and headed inside.

Pissed, Lynch grabbed me by my arm. "Do you understand me?"

I jerked my arm back and headed inside. "You can kiss my ass on this."

We entered the Senate Committee hearing room, which was cold, impersonal, and mostly void of people as it was a special closed-door session already in progress.

The Sergeant at Arms showed us to our seats, which were in front of microphones directly in front of the tribunal. I sat next to Kevin in the front. Lynch and the Clayborn BioMedical CEO fell in behind us.

A bailiff rose and approached Kevin and me. "Do you swear to tell the truth, the whole truth and nothing but the truth, so help you, God?"

I turned toward Lynch before answering. I took a moment. "I do."

Kevin, worried, glared at me.

The official, Senator Candies, glowered toward Kevin and me. "Dr. Palmer, Dr. Winfield; you're late."

I smiled as I sat. "Traffic was..."

Senator Candies cut me off and fired back with both barrels. "You need to tell me why we shouldn't pull your funding."

"Because, with this program, we will save the government billions of taxpayers dollars. Money that can be spent on homeland security."

"At what cost?" Senator Candies wiped his chin as if he was Auguste Rodin's The Thinker.

His remark caused me to think of the lab's procedure room where Matchit, a Native American, forty-years-old, sat at an interrogation desk with his hands cuffed, and his feet shackled. A guard stood watch behind him.

"Dr. Palmer, are you with us?" Senator Candie's eyes seemed as if they turned red.

"Our federal government spends seventy-five billion dollars a year on incarceration programs."

Senator Candies crossed his arms over his chest. "Money isn't everything."

I looked like a deer in headlights.

"It's not about the monetary cost to the government, but the physical cost to the individual."

I scratched my head as I drew a deep breath to think about my next response. "With all due respect, as a nation, I don't feel we can afford not to use this program."

Unsympathetic, Senator Candies smirked a wicked grin. "I was one of the program's biggest supporters, but I don't like being ambushed on national television right before an election. So frankly, after the reports I received this morning, the Rico event looks like the good part."

Oh, the Rico part. Do you remember when Rico threw a stranger in front of a fast-moving train? What this meant to me was that the Senator unveiled the fact that Lynch tried to maximize the company's profits.

I looked down as my thoughts returned to the lab.

***

A Lab Tech unbuttoned Matchit's shirt and removed it, exposing the Native American.

"Holy shit! Look at that." The lab tech's heart raced as he gazed at Matchit's fully covered body of Indian themed tattoos and scars.

Matchit's looked like a cross between Frankenstein and a badass warrior. Pieces of flesh looked like they were ripped off and stapled back on and then woven into his tattoos. Not an inch on his back, shoulders, or chest was spared.

The lab tech removed a knit hat from Matchit's head. "Oh, fuck!"

Matchit's long hair was cut into a mohawk like what an Indian warrior might sport if he went berserk. His head looked like it had been scalped. Cratered looking scars covered his bald-headed dome, and it appeared as if someone peeled away parts of his skin, and then reattached it from other areas to wrap his head.

The lab tech gasped. "Man look at this guy. I've never seen anything like this." He ran his finger through Matchit's hair. "This is so gross, look at this."

I pressed my lips against the microphone. "Knock it off."

***

Back in the Senate hearing, Kevin leaped to his feet to intercede. "What happened in the lab had nothing to do with this project. The television reports are way overblown and not connected. The CDC and FDA reports make it clear there are no causal connections. It's the fourth tab in your package."

The Senator leaned back and flipped through the tabs in the report.

Kevin and I had the momentum. I seized the moment and took up the cause. "We have done everything to ensure the safety of all nonviolent prisoners."

Senator Candies slammed the package of notes down onto his desk. "Sitting here listening to you and finding out what I did this morning, I just don't believe you." He cleared his throat. "Six months ago, you stated, there were no reports of any issues. You also stated that there were zero problems with the program. Then you reported three months ago that there were no post-confinement problems of any kind. I find out yesterday that none of this is true."

Kevin pressed his hands against the table. "There might have been a few technical issues."

Senator Candies shook his head as he diverted his eyes toward me. "Dr. Palmer, I'll ask you one more time. What happened in the lab yesterday?"

I looked back at Lynch. My mind traveled back to the lab, as Kevin said, "But, no real problems."

***

Kevin and I observed the procedure from the control room. He briefly stood in a defensive posture. "But no real problems."

I glanced over to him. "We're ready to begin."

The lab tech stared at Matchit's shoulder tattoo, which consisted of an Indian scalping a White guy bound by his hands and feet and stretched as far as possible.

65

When Zachary flipped the switch, it caused Matchit to scream. In Matchit's drug dream world, a large bowie knife cut across his scalp and pulled back as if ripped from his head. Matchit grimaced in pain. "Ahhhhhhh!"

Inside of Matchit's dream world, he was scalped and bound like the White man in his tattoo. The White man played with his Bowie knife after his hair was peeled off and then he carved down Matchit's chest as Matchit stifled his screams.

Smiling, the White Man carved a second line an inch over, but parallel. He took his time and enjoyed the moment.

Matchit grimaced but kept his composure. It was a battle to see who gave first. The White guy sliced across the top of the two cuts. Then he used the knife as a pry bar, grabbed Matchit's scalp and slowly peeled it away.

Matchit's grimace turned into a horrifying scream as the White guy enjoyed his victory.

Was this victory? Matchit twitched and moaned.

Matchit strained the moment the drug coursed through his veins, but the stress caused him to experience a Grand Mal seizure. Suddenly, Matchit woke up and slowly became enraged. His eyes turned crimson as if they filled by blood.

Inside the monitoring station, Abby panicked as the brain map quickly became bright red, and the pituitary area turned purple, and then black. The E.E.G. machine went crazy.

Inside the procedure room, Matchit flopped uncontrollably to get out of the restraints. One of the arm restraints failed.

Kevin slammed his fist onto the red alarm button. "Put another strap on that right arm!"

The lab tech raced to follow Kevin's order. Right before he strapped the buckle, a guard entered. Matchit grabbed the guard and threw him across his body. The guard sailed ten feet through the air, hitting the wall. Matchit caught hold of lab tech and squeezed his throat, cutting off his breath. Matchit broke his other arm free and unbuckled his chest strap.

Alarms blared as Matchit's readings ricocheted off the chart. I hit a second alarm button. Abby struggled to get a key into a drug lockbox.

Matchit placed the lab tech into a headlock, grabbed the syringe from the I.V. port and used it as a knife. He sliced the lab tech's face.

Agony befell the lab tech who screamed in agony. His face pumped blood as his veins exploded before my eyes.

With the help of everyone else, they pinned Matchit arms down. Matchit leaned over and bit a chunk of the lab tech's face off.

The lab tech covered his face. "Casey!"

I felt the panic in the lab tech's tone and bolted to the procedure room. Kevin raced into it too rushed into too and punched Matchit in his face.

He loosened his bite on the lab tech's face. Matchit grabbed the wound and tore a piece of the lab tech's flesh away from his face with his hands as lab tech screamed in agony.

Kevin began to hyperventilate in a panic. "Where's security?"

I struggled to restrain Matchit from doing more harm to the lab tech and others.

Abby rushed in, removing a cap from a needle. "Hold him still!"

Suddenly, Matchit realized he must stop Abby from stabbing him with the syringe. He grabbed a guard by the throat and squeezed him tighter.

Abby watched in horror as the guard turned blue. She jabbed Matchit with the needle and administered twenty ccs of Thorazine.

It didn't affect Matchit in the least.

Abby grabbed the guard and attempted to wrestle him away from Matchit's firm grasp. The guard's eyes bulged as the Thorazine started to work on Matchit who fell unconscious. The guard also fell to the floor choking unable to breathe. The other lab tech clutched his face in agony.

A guard burst into the room.

Kevin trembled in panic. "Stop!"

The guard charged Matchit. "It's over!"

I needed to find out what set Matchit off. How did he become so violent? Was it the military formula causing the reaction, or was it something I overlooked? I needed to know.

***

Back in the hearing room, Senator Candies slammed the gavel. "Dr. Palmer!"

Kevin interrupted the rest of the sentence. "I think…"

"…Thank you, Dr. Winfield, but I was talking to Dr. Palmer, not you. Dr. Palmer, why should we let this project go forward?"

Casey cleared his throat, holding back his temper. "The issue in the lab had nothing to do with the nonviolent prisoner program, and it certainly did not happen in my lab.

68

If we only administered the drug to nonviolent offenders, there is no problem with Neuro Confinement."

Senator Candies acted as if he foamed from the mouth like a rabid dog. "So, what happened? Explain it to me so that I clearly understand the ramifications."

Kevin covered the microphone and leaned into my ear to whisper to me in private. "Don't go there; he's fishing."

I turned to look at Lynch, and then toward the CEO who stared inquisitively at me.

Senator Candies rubbed his temples. "So, let me ask you this. Why should we change the current program that has been in place for a few hundred years?"

I came unhinged. "Are you fucking kidding?"

"Excuse me, Dr. Palmer." The Senator pointed his index finger toward me. "I don't like where this is going."

I felt a pit in my stomach form. "The current system is broken, and you know it! So, face it. We have to do something rather than sit on a fat senatorial ass."

"How dare you talk to me like that? You're out of line. I control this hearing, not you."

I was too worked up to care. "You talk about the cost to the individual, what about the cost to the family and society? It can't be much worse than what we have!"

Senator Candies exploded by slamming his fist against the table. "So, if your system works so well, explain the dead inmate."

I tried to calm myself, realizing things were heading downhill and getting out of hand. "As I said, that had nothing to do with the nonviolent prisoner program."

Senator Candies pressed me again. "So, what happened in the lab yesterday? Explain that to me in a nonviolent way."

I lifted from my chair as Kevin grabbed me preventing me from moving, so I sat before I answered the Senator's last question. "Seventy-seven percent of convicted felons are back in prison within five years. They aren't rehabilitated. It rips families apart. In our program less than five percent return to prison. Don't you see that as successful?"

Senator Candies looked like a smoothing pile of embers. "Are you going to tell me what happened in the lab, or not?"

My temper flared, and so did my voice. "Bullshit like this, from people like you, is why nothing gets done."

Senator Candies whacked his gavel. "This panel is recessed, thanks for making my decision extremely clear for me."

I swallowed hard. "Senator! Senator! Wait!"

He spun and stared at me. "I will find out."

I did not doubt that he would as I waited in the back hallway of the Justice building.

Kevin exited the chamber with the CEO and handed him a sizeable overstuffed file. They talked, but I was too far away to hear. The CEO left.

I approached Kevin. "What in Hell was that about?"

"You did well and adhered to my advice."

"I could've done better."

Kevin placed his arm around my shoulder. "You did fine."

He did care.

CHAPTER SIX

Casey's Mind Space

Everywhere your eyes darted, thick oblivious whiteness made it absurdly difficult to see; blinding really, welcome to my world of self-induced Neuro Confinement. I fabricated this -- a construct of my mind where I sat on a white leather overstuffed chair. Everything in here was a slight Dahlesque which meant it looked like it had leaped out of a bright-colored Dali painting pulsating as if everything took to life.

Technically, by definition, it was alive as it was the representation of my thoughts plugged into a construct that I could understand. The words were superficial compared to what was in here where I was free to create. I was always at ease with myself in there. However, at times, it resembled an emotional storm of immense proportions where my thoughts rolled around in the background, and then slowly formed into a stream of consciousness.

Other times, thoughts and images emerged from nowhere, and I forced them to form through deliberate

71

thought provocations and consideration. My mind was indeed an exciting place for me to work, although it took me a while to get used to this constant boil of soft-low almost a murmur of voices. The voices never stopped, which occupied my mind to a certain amount of aggravation. A few times, they became overwhelming, and I couldn't stop them until I left that world. Even now, I heard them in my real world, which became a little unsettling.

The voices always murmured and rambled as they worked out equations, theories, and other scientific topics. My only rest from the quantum chaos was when the voices discussed where to go for lunch. When I focused hard, I could listen to them as if I spoke with an old friend. Upon hindsight, the voices represented different versions of my other personalities which surfaced sporadically. I would stop short of calling them different people, but you could think of them that way. I know I do.

Think of this place as a vast sea of thoughts, memories, and images. On both sides of this space in the recesses of my mind were hundreds of floating numbers, formulas, equations, pictures, thoughts, and even memories that covered the vast whiteness. The inside was a tempest but still controlled. Blueish electrical pulses fired and traveled down these lines regularly. Everything was connected by thin blue lines running in multiple directions joining everything. Thoughts shot like lightning bolts where hundreds of neurons fired at one time. The pulses raced down the power lines until they reached the spot in front of my chair. I learned not to venture into the matrix of my thoughts as I once did, which required adapting to my environment.

When I began my mind matrix, I decided to try to find the edges. First, I must say I don't think they exist because it was not three dimensional. We tried to use words to give us a point of reference, but when you feel you're in one spot, in a blink, you could be somewhere totally different.

The part that was disconcerting was what I called the Dark Matrix. I was swept up into it that first time. To picture the Dark Matrix, think of thick, sticky tar that held your nightmare together in one spot. If you had ever been on a bad trip and you pleaded with God promising Him, you would never do whatever you did again, that was child's play compared to this. The energy could tear you apart, or the memories could scar you for life.

My first time into the matrix, I started walking beneath the representation of my thoughts. A thought fired off as I approached. Seeing the thought form was incredible as it took energy to morph. They arrived as particles that merged into a picture. Sometimes it was a note of music or a single thought that developed. The first image or picture or whatever it was, I called the seed.

Moreover, like any seed, it grew as it traveled around in my brain. Think of it like a dragster slowing, taking off, and then hitting the gas pedal steadily until you're doing three hundred miles per hour. That's how these thoughts propelled inside my mind. That was cool. It gave me a new perspective on how I thought. However, it just wasn't worth the pain. As I walked, I noticed I was no longer on the ground but flying inside of the matrix. It was an outstanding effect as gravity disappeared and I became weightless. I floated in space. However, each time a thought formed around me, a bolt of electricity went through me, burning and searing my soul. Imagine as if millions of volts of electricity zapped you. Every synapse of your body opened at once when this happened.

The pain was mammoth and off the chart. If you had ever seen a mosquito fried by a bug zapper, that was what it felt like your body sizzling like a charred remnant of its former self. The procedure made me sore for days, and worse, I couldn't get rid of the smell of searing flesh. Anything that happened in the matrix, you felt and reacted to it as if real. Then if that wasn't enough, I was immediately thrown down a blue filament tumbling like a tumbleweed bouncing into anything and everything, and when you struck a memory -- wow! It made you instantly feel that sensation. The feeling was stronger than anything you had ever felt before. Just imagine if you had to live each thought. Not just think about it, but you became the thought. It was overwhelming, and words cannot describe this feeling. It was so much vivid and real than when it happened.

Time was frozen for me every night here -- a free-floating Dahlesque melting clock with a red second hand that didn't move floated to my right. That was my anchor, and when it moved, I only had seconds before I was cast back into reality. I had a way of keeping focused for hours and days at a time. I used my mind time for a year's worth of research every single night. Just imagine if you could focus on a problem for years at a time how much would you get done. Think about it. When I didn't stop for breaks, food, water, go to the bathroom, or sleep, I accomplished major feats in my research. How? Those activities are useless in the matrix because they were not needed, and I focused like a laser beam homed in on any problem I wished to address. Most found this unbearable, but I found it comforting. Through the years, I discovered a way to control the process, and I didn't let it control me.

I had calculated that I spent over nine hundred years inside Neuro Confinement logging over nine hundred mind years. Mind time equated to one month, which was equal to approximately one year of mind time. My world had expanded so much from where I started. In the beginning, I was lost and even frozen in place. Most people spoke of their frozen experience. It took me years to escape the clutches of that deep freeze. Now I traveled anywhere in my mind that I wanted. It had been invaluable to my research.

Also, I could build my world if I visualized it hard enough. However, those activities and brain waves drained me. It zapped my energy, and it could take you a day or two of real-time to recover from it. Usually, I did what I called reconstructed experiences, where I built new worlds, creating unique and original experiences and obtained new skills. I think they didn't take as much brainpower as when I constructed them from scratch. I knew they were easier on my body and mind. If you created a new spin on a place you already knew, then it could be quite easy to finish it out. One time I constructed a city, but it turned into a labyrinth, and I became lost in it for days. At the time, I was on a super dose. I no longer dosed myself to that level because when things happened in there, I perceived them as real. Sometimes I struggled to make it back to the real world.

However, tonight, I was on a mission to prove that one of my theories should have worked, but instead, my thinking became erratic. *What the hell went wrong?* I questioned why my thinking was that far off. *How could this be?* I proved it over and over many ways, and I had lots of safeguards to guarantee against those issues. Anyway, I became obsessed and enthralled with my logic.

To my immediate left were many oddball items. In front of them was a young girl. That's my daughter, Julie, a steady six-years-old. She sat and played jacks quietly by herself. It warmed my heart to see her, which kept me wanting to maintain myself in the Dark Matrix. At least this way I see her every night. She always smiled in there and was happy to be with me. She knew I had to conduct my research, so she helped me when she could. However, mostly, she comforted me by being there next to me. I missed her so much in the real world that it hurt.

In front of me hovered a long, complex equation connected by a blue strand. I stared at it for a second and added an integer. The formula calculated as Julie's voice estimated the success rate. "The likelihood of success is seventy-one percent."

The bluish-white light struck like far off lightning eventually making it to the thin blue line of the equation. It was a ball of electricity that entered the equation as the answer turned red and vaporized. I pondered the outcome. I rocked back and forth as I moved the equation around and added a new integer. It recalculated with a strike of bluish-white light from far off. One of my voices estimated the success rate. "The likelihood of success is ninety-one percent."

The answer illuminated green. Pleased, I added another complex formula as Julie watched.

She pursed her lips. "The likelihood of success is one hundred percent."

I became perturbed. "It should've worked. How can this be? No matter how I calculated the formula, the outcome is the same. Am I missing something? What has changed to make it go haywire?" I thought hard to check myself and produced another equation. My mind recalculated, and all of it pulsed green. *Shit! I must be missing something.*

Julie twisted her lips in frustration as she crinkled her freckled nose. "Daddy, you promised me you would watch your language."

I smiled and huffed a deep sigh of relief. "I'm sorry, sweetheart, you're right." I took another deep breath and returned to my work.

What if it was contaminated? Did I run a diagnostic on the formula?

I retrieved a complex, slowly spinning molecule and manipulated part of the structure by adding a carbon molecule. The compound slowly rotated as Julie estimated the success rate. "The likelihood of success is seventy-four point eight hundred and twenty percent." It glowed white, graduated to red, and then slowly vaporized.

I shook my head and clenched my jaw. "Fuck, this doesn't make sense."

Julie's eyes widened. "Daddy!"

I looked at Julie for a moment, drew in a deep breath and pulled up a new complex equation adding several integers to it. The lightning storm sizzled and buzzed as it recalculated the equation.

Julie began to estimate the success rate. "The like... ly hooooood... ...f suc... ccc..." Her voice drug from a staccato to a stop. All the other voices sped up then, and then abruptly stopped.

Julie sang as she stood and twirled. "Ring-a-ring-the-roses, a pocket full of posies."

The red second hand on the clock thundered as it slowly started to move.

Julie continued to twirl. "Ashes! Ashes!"

A three in the equation liquefied and puddled on the ground.

Julie made her final spin. "We all fall down. Bye for now, Daddy."

Several other numbers puddled to the ground. The floor melted and disappeared as everything fell into a black abyss. As each item dropped, everything darkened until blackness encapsulated the Dark Matrix followed by a loud thud.

I woke up in my living room; all the colors in the room were back to normal, and I was alone. I breathed heavy. I sat up, leaned forward on the edge of the chair, and looked around. It took a second to gather my thoughts. I pulled out my notebook and studied several formulas. I scratched them out. *"Fuck! I was there!"* Then out of frustration, I ripped the entire page from my notebook and tossed it across the room onto the floor.

Splat!

CHAPTER SEVEN

To the Firing Squad

There was a thorn in my side, and his name was Zachary Thomas. He was thirty years old, thin, and waspy. He tensely waited in the Clayborn BioMedical break room as if ready to attack. I entered, and Zachary immediately frowned. "You look like shit."

I ignored his flagrant comment and poured myself a cup of coffee. He could be a bit of an asshole. However, today, my head was killing me. I downed a large gulp of day-old coffee and swallowed four ibuprofens.

Zachary took that opportunity to get beneath my skin and grate me. "Thought you were taking some time off?

"Are you trying to piss me off or is there a point to this?" I ran my hand through my hair while craning my head back and squirted some eye drops to relieve my bloodshot eyes.

Zachary held up a letter. He thought he got to me or something. "What about your time off to travel the world? You must have pissed them off. They're pulling your funding." Zachary looked back at the letter.

I held my tongue for a moment before I headed for the door. I smelled him. "You're really are an asshole."

"And, they want all of your files." Zachary smirked full of jealousy.

I stopped just short of the door. "What?"

Zachary grinned with accomplishment. "Including your precious little notebooks."

I grabbed the letter from Zachary.

Zachary enjoyed the gotcha-moment with a flip of his hand.

I ignored his arrogant move. I wanted to say something. However, he was not worth my breath. I crumpled the paper and shoved it into Zachary's shirt pocket. I patted him on his chest. "Stick it up your ass." I walked out and headed to Kevin's office.

As I turned the corner, I ran into a load of people. I waded through them and stopped at Kevin's door. I peeped in, and he was working at his neat and tidy desk.

I looked around at all the people in the hall with curiosity and, then my eyes landed on Kevin. "Who are all these people?"

"The powers at large decided to change several policies." Kevin exhaled, returning his focus to his paperwork.

"Which policies?"

Kevin glanced at his watch. "We're late for a meeting with Lynch."

"You're not going to answer me, are you?"

"Just remember, I'm on your side."

"Why do I suddenly feel like you're bringing me to a firing squad?"

"Something like that." Kevin flashed a fake-as-they-come smile as he exited.

I followed in his footsteps as we continued down the hallway and then stopped at a security door. I swiped my card and pulled on the door to open it. It didn't work. This place needed to update its entire system. I took my card and rubbed it on my pants to see if that would make it work.

Kevin reached up and swiped his card. "Here." The door opened.

We entered the laboratory conference room where Lynch was seated at the head of the table. Next to Todd sat Griffen, the stern CEO, who was in his early sixties and was charismatic. Several others surrounded the table. Lynch cleared his throat. "Gentlemen, please take a seat. We have a few more changes to make."

We sat as Lunch continued to speak. "Kevin will become the point man for the new program. We are combining the labs for now. Casey's team will merge with Kevin's. That's all, Kevin, I need to talk to you and Casey."

Everyone else but Lynch, Kevin, Casey, and Todd left. The CEO coldly stared at me. "Casey, the new program doesn't need you."

I lifted one brow confused. "That's fine, but you can't have my formula."

Kevin smirked a wry grin. "Thought he could do the research?"

Todd shook his head. "You changed the formula, recently didn't you?" He fixated on me.

His remark and the way he gawked at me sent me through the roof; figuratively, of course. "You trying to blame me for Matchet?"

81

Lynch licked his lips. "The board thinks the change in formula is why the inmate went into psychosis."

My face turned red, and the muscles throughout my body stiffened. "That's bullshit; the program was never meant for violent criminals. I can't even get any information about who some of these prisoners are, much less why they are in my program!"

Todd scratched his ear. "We are not going to get into a debate with you, and you were supposed to fix the formula. That didn't happen, so you're out until after the investigation is over!"

I bit the interior of my cheek to maintain my composure. "Fine! Then I'm pulling the drug." I stormed toward the door.

Todd stood as if he was about to come after me. "You can't do that."

My feet felt like cement as I stopped in my tracks and gradually turned toward Lynch. "I can, and I will."

Todd drew in a slow deep breath as he puffed his chest like a mad dog out of control. "We classified your work and the drug as a national security secret six months ago to ensure the prisoner drug vote. You only own it in the title; it's a national security project now."

I glowered back at Lynch more red-faced than before, and I felt the heat escaping from my scalp. "When you brought me on,you told me I kept all the rights to my drug!"

Lynch averted my gaze as if he didn't want to confront me. "You need to reread your contract."

"My contract? What are you talking about?" My heart pounded. I could feel the blood pump in my veins. "When you got the payout for the vote, you signed the rider for national security implications." Lynch held up the contract and read from it. "Any and all rights and future profits are reverted to the company in perpetuity for this payment."

Kevin slammed his fist against the table. I thought he would shatter it. "Whoa! Wait, we need Casey for this project to be successful. Are you trying to sabotage it?"

Todd smacked his lips in disgust. "The decision has been made. Casey has been terminated and has no rights to the research or the drug."

"You know what? Fuck you!" Closed fisted, I punched the wall leaving a small dent. "You're not taking my drug or my work! I'll blow the lid off this mother fucker." I bolted from the room and slammed the door on my way out. At any second, I felt as if a rabid dog's foam would ooze from my mouth and nostrils. I knew there was no point in arguing with Lynch or with the CEO. Last time I did that, the guards had to pull me off Todd.

Kevin rushed after me.

Todd nodded confidently. "So now we ramp up the prisoner program to twice the old levels."

"What about Candies?" Lynch rubbed his forehead.

"He'll do his song and dance for the cameras, but it won't change anything. He owes me right now."

"And the funds?"

Todd smiled. "Five million now and the rest in ninety days assuming you can keep the volume up."

***

Kevin pushed his way through a line of prisoners.

I entered the lab with Kevin at my heels. I turned to Kevin with fervor. "I can't believe you did that."

"I didn't have any other choice. They must do this, or we lose the funding."

"I am so pissed right now." I held my tongue; it's not Kevin's fault. I began to clean out my stuff.

As I grabbed my notebooks, he grabbed my arm. "I need your codes and keys."

I turned to Kevin and laughed. "Figure it out your fucking self. You guys are smart. Shouldn't take more than, a hundred and twenty years because that's about how long it took me." I quickly scanned the office and spotted a box of paper and dumped it on the floor. I started jamming all my stuff inside.

As I put my things into the box, Kevin removed them. "They don't want you to take anything. They say it's all company property."

"I can't believe this bullshit." I stopped and looked at Kevin. "Their property? Their property my ass." I continued and swiped the photo of my wife and daughter off the wall.

Kevin grabbed the picture and bowed up to me. "They said everything."

A twisted and weird look formed across my face. Kevin knew this look as a creased formed on my brow. "This box and my dead family members are coming with me unless they're planning on killing me." At times, I think I scared him. I was on the verge of going into a rage. Kevin realized this and backed down.

I started to leave with the small box of things when I spotted Lynch on the other side of the lab door staring at me. I swiped my pass to open the door, but it didn't work. *How could I have not caught this earlier?*

Lynch smiled as he enjoyed the moment. "You need to drop everything, or you don't leave."

Frozen for a moment, I contemplated my next words very carefully. "As I said before, fuck you!" I grabbed the nearest massive thing near me, a computer monitor, and I heaved it toward Lynch. The monitor bounced off the re-enforced Lexan door.

In a rage, I ripped through the lab like a Tasmanian devil.

Kevin tried to calm me down with futile results. "This isn't going to help?"

The chair received my attention. I tossed it toward the door. "Makes me feel better!" My middle finger proudly shot him the bird.

Kevin grabbed me by my arms. "You need to cool off."

I fended him off, grabbed a telephone, and then flung it at the door.

Kevin grabbed me again and shook me. "You need to stop."

"You're right, you're right. I do need to cool off." I took a deep, cleansing breath.

Kevin released me, and then I slowly and calmly strode to the far wall. "This should do it." Like a child having a temper tantrum, I smashed the fire alarm button.

Sprinklers of halon spray spewed as the emergency lights flashed. I grabbed my box and yanked on the locked door. I turned to Kevin. "I didn't think you would be a fucking traitor! Let me out of this place."

Kevin stared at me, and I thought for a moment, he might have felt guilty. He looked at Lynch, stared at him, and then looked back at me. He snatched his badge and unlocked the door.

As Lynch's face turned redder than mine, I yanked the door open. I stormed out, stopping at Lynch. I wanted to say something but decide not to, and I marched out right past him with my shit.

The front door of the building wasn't that far, but I fumed all the way out and jumped into my 1970s beater pickup truck. I blankly stared at the steering wheel before I pounded it with both fists. "Fuck! Shit! Fuck! Fuck you all!"

I placed a call to Clayborn Biomedical. As I waited for the secretary to answer, I studied my family's photo.

"Clayborn Biomedical. How may I direct your call?"

"Kevin Winfield, please."

"I'm sorry, but that building is evacuating due to a fire alarm."

"Can I leave a message for him?"

"Yes, you may. What is it?"

"This is Redbone, tell him I'm sorry, and I'll meet him at the usual place at eight tonight. He'll know." I drummed my pencil against my notebook. I opened the back of the frame to my family's photograph and pulled out a sheet which had all my passwords and codes handwritten on it. I didn't know why I kept those much less why I hid them because I remembered them all.

CHAPTER EIGHT

Old Friends and New Enemies

I had been drinking since the afternoon, and it was evident by my slurred words and sluggish behavior. I sat in one of my favorite dive bars, the Old Abstinence Bar downtown. This place was fantastic, and it reminded me of my dad's old heavy leather furniture. The bar looked and felt like something out of the Prohibition days. I think that the twenties and thirties were my favorite eras.

My first car was a Model A Ford. I used to pretend I was Clyde Barrow and my second-best friend, Abby Grace, my meek now lab assistant, was Bonnie Parker. We'd drink cheap gin on picnics down by the river. Kevin even sported a zoot suit when he tagged along. Abby and I were never a couple, but I think she wanted us to be one.

This bar's art deco abstinence fountain sat at one end of the bar, and house-made tinctures in small brown bottles littered the back bar. It had an eclectic, yet cozy feel to it. The bartender finished making me a cocktail called Death in the Afternoon, which was Ernest Hemingway's favorite. It was a risky pairing of jigger absinthe and iced champagne. The proper amount of champagne in this concoction was when the cocktail turned an opalescent milky-white. I must admit that the licorice and champagne flavor took a while for me to acquire the taste. However, Hemingway drank three to four of these in one sitting, trying not to kill himself.

Today, I think I am forging toward a record in my consumption. I reminisced about growing up with Kevin and spilled my guts to the bartender. "Kevin told everyone I tied him to a kite!" I made gestures which insinuated the size of the kite. "It was twelve feet tall, and he told everyone I pushed him." The memories of us flooded my brain.

"Did he?" The bartender wiped the rim of a glass with his dirty rag.

My focus was on my memories. It was like I was reliving my life but in a slightly different version of it. That was when Abby passed her hand in front of my face.

"Hello, anyone in there?" She waved her hand again.

I laughed. "Sorry I forgot where I was for a moment."

The bartender set the glass down on the counter. "Well, did you push him?" He made me another drink.

"Oh, Hell, no! He yelled Geronimo and then jumped."

The bartender handed me another Death in the Afternoon, and a took a sip.

Kevin approached from behind me. "He did break my arms."

Abby wiggled her button nose. "They were inseparable until Casey fell in love with somebody else."

I glanced toward Abby as I held my drink up. "Were you jealous?"

Abby shook her head no as I downed my drink in one

swig. The liquid burned as it coursed down my throat. "You were jealous?"

"No, I was happy for you."

I could tell I hurt her feelings by the solemn expression that twisted her lips. However, she would never say it, and I knew it.

The bartender prepared me another drink. "So, the three of you were best friends?"

Kevin shook his head in affirmation. "You could say that."

I smiled a slow grin. "Yeah, best friend that fucks me out of a job."

Kevin glared toward me. "Oh, that's cold."

Abby put one hand on each on Kevin's and Casey's shoulder. "I wasn't even there."

Kevin grabbed Casey around the neck. "I love this guy; Casey is like a brother to me. He lies like a son of a bitch, though."

The bartender laughed.

Casey pursed his lips. "What are we going to do about my drug?"

The bartender laughed as he handed Casey another drink.

Kevin smiled at the bartender. "Come on, Casey, let's sit at a quiet table."

I nodded in agreement and Abby, and I followed him to a corner table.

Kevin plopped down onto the chair. "I'm gonna getcha your job back."

I sat across from him and then sloshed my drink around. "Fuck the job. What are we going to do about my drug?"

"We, ain't doing nothing. Lynch wanted to arrest you for destroying the office. I think I've talked him out of it."

"Fuck him; he's nothing but a cocksucker."

"One step at a time, buddy." Kevin crossed his arms over his chest.

I downed the rest of my drink. "So, I just go away, and they steal my shit?"

Kevin shook his head, frustrated instead of answering.

I stared at him for a moment. "Can you at least get me an appointment with Candies?"

Kevin melted because he knew where I was going with this conversation. "What, you're going for the jugular now?"

I beamed with pride. "If they think they have problems now, just wait. I'm not going to let them get away with this."

Kevin hung his head low. "There's more. I'm waiting for it. Zachary is taking over what's left of your team."

"I knew when he stopped me in the break room, something was up. That little shit is going to get someone else killed." I clenched my jaw.

Kevin waved at the bartender to get his attention. He grabbed Casey's glass, held it up and pointed, indicating he wanted three more.

One of the bar's patrons, Cassandra Reed, nonchalantly watched and listened from the corner.

Kevin went into protection mode. "So what? They're convicts."

He knew how I felt about this, and now he pushed my buttons.

The bartender approached carrying the three drinks on a tray.

I couldn't contain myself any longer. I was more than fed up; I was furious. "Next thing you're going to say is they're all guilty."

Kevin nodded. "Yeah."

"You're a heartless bastard; I should leave."

Kevin stood almost bumping into the bartender who placed the tray on the table. Kevin shook his head in disappointment. "Don't bother, stay, and drink. That's what you're good at." He slammed his chair against the table and quickly exited.

If I hadn't been drunk at the time, I would have beat him to the punch and left.

Cassandra smiled as Kevin left. She eyed me and flashed a wry grin.

Abby took notice of my frustration. "You okay?"

I stared at Cassandra and avoided Abby's eyes. "How long have they been running violent offenders?"

"Look, they tell me less than they tell you."

"So, you're not going to tell me anything either?"

Abby gathered her stuff. "Anyway, I need to get going. I have to pick up my daughter from the babysitter's." She hugged me. "You need a ride home?"

"No." My eyes remained glued on Cassandra.

"You let them get to you too easily." Abby smiled and left.

I waved goodbye with my half-empty glass.

I continued to stare at Cassandra and decided to make a move. I stumbled up to her and plopped down in a seat next to her. "Don't I know you?"

"I don't think we have ever met." Cassandra extended her hand, and we shook.

"I'm Casey, Casey Palmer. I know you from somewhere. Give me a minute, and I'll figure it out. I may forget a name, but I never forget a face."

She lifted her brow. "What would you like to drink?"

"What you have seems to be working."

I lifted my glass toward the bartender.

Cassandra watched my every move. "Which of society's ills are you solving?"

I looked at her for a moment. "For-profit prisons."

Cassandra frowned perplexedly. "Entrapment of the human soul?"

I laughed because I think I liked this woman. "That's one way to put it. I've sold mine." I took a gulp of my drink, enjoying the taste as it quenched my thirst. "Have you ever been in prison?"

Cassandra laughed while shaking her head. "Put in prison? Gosh, no. However, I've visited people in prison numerous times."

I swirled my almost empty glass and then pointed with my index finger. "I bet you don't know that sixty-seven and a half percent of released prisoners were rearrested within three years. Almost fifty-two percent wind up back in prison." I poked her gently on her chest.

"So, you're saying prison doesn't work?"

"Yep, not just doesn't work. The recidivism rates proved that it's a waste of effort and resources." At this point, I'm slurring my words.

"Curious, so how do you propose to fix it?"

I started to take a sip as it a thought hit me. "I think we..." Casey's eyes widened. "Fuck, now I know where I've seen you before. I watched you on television. You were the chick busting Candies' balls on Fox news."

Cassandra handed me her business card.

Instantly, my buzz waned, and I studied the card that read -- "Cassandra Reid, Project Freedom." My mood suddenly went to stone-cold asshole.

Cassandra toasted me with her drink. I couldn't believe this fuckin bitch. I became agitated and felt bamboozled. I glared her straight into her eyes as if I were a dragon ready to spit fire. "So, you're here to fuck me for information?"

Cassandra shook her head. "I don't need to; I learned a lot from your interaction with your buddies. Observance is a powerful thing when you want to obtain information. I must confess, I learned more over the last ten minutes, give or take a few than in the last few years." She sipped her cocktail as she cut her eyes toward me and curling her upper lip into a straight smile.

"Are you stalking me or something?" I stepped back because I want to view her entire body language. I needed to figure out what drove this woman and why she was stalking me.

"I wouldn't call it stalking, yet." She winked and fluttered her long lashes.

Is she flirting with me? I looked at the bartender. "What do I owe you, Mike?"

"Fifty-seven fifty."

I grabbed a wad of cash from my pocket and started to peel off several twenties. "Fuck it." I flicked a small wad onto the table. I inched closer to Cassandra so that I could whisper in her ear and leaned into her. "Fuck you."

"Fuck me? Whatcha think? Do you honestly think they are going to be loyal to you? It sounds like you're the one that got bent over and prodded without the benefit of Vaseline."

Boy, she was sharp. If I weren't so pissed, I might like her. I downed the rest of my drink. "I don't have any comment, and before I'm on the six o'clock news, bite me." I pointed my middle finger toward her.

She smiled like she had won something.

I headed for the door. "See you, Mike."

Cassandra rose seething on the inside. "I know about D-214!"

"How does a civilian know about this?"

"It must be stopped!"

I looked back over my shoulder, stared at her, then thundered through the door -- pissed.

CHAPTER NINE

You Won't Like Me If I'm Angry

Meanwhile, back at the lab, an inmate named Stricker, mid-fifties, and a scrawny-bug-eyed man stared at the floor. Striker was a broken man who led a hard life.

Zachary was ready to get the procedure over. He cleared his throat. "Name?"

Stricker remained fixated in his stare; he was in his other world.

Zachary exhaled with more force. "What's your name?"

Striker continued his gaze at the floor.

Zachary, annoyed, clicked his tongue. "Look I've had a rough day, if you fuck with me, I'm going to make you suffer. What's your name, asshole?"

Striker remained unphased.

Frustrated, a lab technician grabbed Striker's wrist band and read the name. "This is R. J. Striker. R.J.? What, you don't have a real first name! With that beak, I'll call you Raven. Ha, you like that?"

Zachary retrieved his clipboard and headed out of the room as he spoke. "Take him in and strap his ass down, really good. I don't want him to be able to move. Let's make this raven fly."

The lab tech tugged on one of Striker's arms. "Come on, let's go."

Striker refused to stand and pulled back, tightening every muscle to become fixed in place.

The lab tech nodded to the guards, and without a verbal command, they drug Striker toward the laboratory procedure room. En route, R.J. urinated splashing it at the feet of each guard.

"What the fuck?" The larger guard, pissed, shoved Striker on his back.

Striker didn't make it easy for them as he became like a dead man rag doll. They yanked him up onto a bench and removed the cuffs and leg irons as the laboratory technician went to work.

The technician smirked. "Fuck this asshole up." He slapped Striker's face. "You're going to be a good boy and cooperate, Okay?"

Striker remained limp as if an overcooked spaghetti noodle that would stick to the ceiling.

The guards hurled him onto the pedestal table, and then sat him up for a long-term stay as they hooked up electrodes and I.V.s to him.

Amazingly, Striker cooperated and sat like a Zombie on Ambien.

Zachary, behind a glass wall in a control room, flipped on computers. He leaned into the microphone. "Quit screwing around. Let's do this thing."

The lab tech through up his hands. "You're not gonna get anything out of him."

"Oh, yes, I will."

The lab tech held up some paper money. "You wanna put a twenty on it?"

"You're on. I'll take a sucker bet any day of the week."

"Look at this guy. I love easy money."

The second lab assistant strapped Striker to the free-floating table with straight jacket looking straps.

Zachary nodded in approval, but a worrisome look crisscrossed his face. He speaks into the mic. "Make sure all those straps are as tight as shit."

The lab tech nodded. "Yazza, boss." He laughed and then moved closer to Striker. "You're a tough guy, huh."

Striker finally upturned his eyes toward the lab tech.

"I'm counting on you." He slapped Striker across his face. "Don't be such a pussy, now."

Striker lowered his head slightly as he seethed.

The lab tech pulled a syringe of Propofol. "This will knock your ass out."

The other technician and guards continued to secure Striker and set him up the procedure instrumentation and medication.

Abby entered the control room and perched in her place at the lab monitoring station.

Zachary's eyes scanned the area, and all of the monitors lit. "Everything is ready. And, we're up. Let's start with forty ccs as a bonus."

Abby looked up as Kevin entered the room.

Kevin's eyes widened. "Hang on a second. I thought we were waiting until we received the new protocols."

"They already revised the protocol." Zachary doubled-checked a procedural list. "Lynch is ramping everything up. For whatever it's worth, this wasn't my idea."

Kevin stepped forward. "What about Casey's limits?"

Zachary grinned ear to ear. "They no longer exist. The new drug is powerful, astonishing results. You will see. You'll feel like a God."

Zachary pushed the call button on his microphone. "Give me five of D-214."

The lab tech pushed five ccs of the drug D-214. "That's forty-five in."

Zachary placed his headphones over his head, so he was the only one listening to the lab tech. "Bombs away."

Kevin's eyes widened in a query. "Only five ccs?"

Amused, Zachary laughed beneath his breath. "Yeah, and the lasers are now able to stop and start the nightmares. When they say they want to be interviewed, hit the switch." Zachary hit the switch and quickly removed his headphones.

Striker screamed in agony, which caught Kevin by surprise.

Zachary chuckled finding Stricker's pain amusing. "You'll get used to the screams. I actually enjoy them now."

Kevin observed Striker through the window.

Zachary's slowly squeezed his fists closed, turning his knuckles white, his breathing increased. "It's like shifting a car." He mimicked shifting a car with four speeds. "Bam."

Striker screamed.

Zachary hit the switch amping the voltage. "Bam."

Striker screamed louder from the pain.

"Bam!" Again, Zachary hit him. "That one is for good measure. It's amazingly effective in obtaining information."

Kevin, unamused, frowned. "Man, I don't know about this, maybe Casey was right."

"Fuck him and the white horse he came in on." Zachary clenched his jaw.

Kevin puffed his chest. "Shut the session down. You are going to overload that man."

Zachary smiled in arrogance. "I no longer work for you; so, fuck off!"

Stunned, Kevin's eyes widened as he felt his blood pressure escalate. "What?"

"You're lucky to have a job after letting Casey leave like that."

"You're a little shit bag." Kevin grabbed Zachary by the collar and pulled him up. "A real dirtbag."

Zachary bowed up. "Touch me again, and you'll be out of here."

Kevin stormed out of the lab.

Zachary proudly watched him leave through the glass viewing window. *I love my work.*

In the lab monitoring station, Abby studied the screen and noticed things were out of kilter. "He's hot on the pineal region. How much did you give him?"

Zachary exhaled exasperatedly not liking Abby questioning him. "I gave him…" He tapped the mic button so the lab tech could hear his answer. "That's forty-five."

The lab tech froze. "That's forty-five more. Damn, that's a lot. You sure?"

Zachary hit the mic button again with a determined voice. "Yep, forty-five is correct." He released the mic switch. "That's what I called for." With a smug smile, Zachary shook and then nodded his head.

The Lab Tech gaped at Zachary for a moment and then administered another forty-five ccs.

Zachary pursed his lips and held his outward laughter, although they found the situation amusing.

Abby tapped the viewing window. "That's too much. Back that down to ten."

Zachary glanced at Striker flashing a wicked smile. "Let's give him ten ccs. That ought to help the situation progress in our favor." He giggled. "Striker, how do you like me now?"

The lab tech hesitated with the syringe in his hand. "Another ten, we're already at ninety, are you insane?" His words fell on deaf ears as only Zachary hear the question and gave a thumbs-up and hits the mic button again.

Zachary shook his head, denying the insanity suggestion, but his grin seemed unmistakably crazy. Ge hit the mic button one more time. He wiped the spit from the corner of his lip. "Give him ten! Will you?"

The lab tech administered another ten ccs. "OK, then; ten more it is. I hope you know what you're doing because you're about to kill him. When push comes to shove, remember I was only following a sick man's orders. I won't be responsible."

Back inside of the laboratory monitoring station, Abby carefully monitored Striker's brain pattern, which rapidly turned red.

Striker's body twitched as if tiny jolts of lightning invaded him. Slowly his veins distended turning purple.

Zachary flashed a confident grin as he gazed upon Stricker's body contort and judder. "Okay, let's get this party started!" With his fingers at the bottom, Zachary hit the button to jolt Striker into his nightmare.

Although Striker was not fully sedated, the purple sludge stuns him awake. His eyes slowly turned red, and then, to purple as his nostrils flared and his breathing became forced. The veins on Striker's neck fully extended and turned purplish as the concoction coursed its way through his body. Striker turned rigid, and then he convulsed.

Multiple monitor alarms blared at once.

Perplexed, Zachary hit numerous switches turning the dials. "What's happening?"

Inside the patient procedure room, the lab assistant shook his head. "Hell, I don't know! It must be from the extra ccs you ordered." *What an idiot.*

Striker continued to seize as his strength intensified breaking free from his straps and began to get off the table. The lab tech tried to restrain him until Striker grabbed around his shoulders and tossed him violently across the room. The lab tech hit the wall like a rag doll. Striker emboldened and naked rose like a phoenix.

The tech gawked at Striker in fear. His throat pinched his words as he trembled.

Zachary hit an emergency call button as Striker tore away all the devices attached to him. He grabbed a phone and frantically dialed. "We need security in here, now!"

Striker watched his reflection in the glass divider and hallucinated that he transformed into a six-foot-bluish-black-raven-headed-angel-of-Death. He pulled his wing to the side of his body, cocooning himself as the transformation took place in his mind.

Three security guards entered grasping tasers.

Striker, drooling, hunched over as if to hide beneath its fabricated wings.

The first Security guard placed his hand on his gun. "Freeze!"

Striker wailed as he thrust his arms and legs out to form an X.

A second security guard stormed toward Striker. "What the Hell are you doing?"

Striker gawked at his hallucinated reflection in the window. In his mind, he saw his ten-foot wingspan fanned out like a peacock's tail plume. He shimmed all over as the feathers rustled with the shake. Striker shook his scrawny naked body and then peered around the lab. *I'm in control now. Look at my fierceness.*

Pop! Pop, pop! The guards fire their tasers into Striker's chest and back. The guards smile as they observed three hundred and twenty thousand volts rip through Striker's body.

Striker seized as he stood. His eyes rolled back into their sockets. His breath quickened with the surge of electricity.

The guards' pleasure turned to horror as Striker's breaths became rhythmic to the point of ecstasy. A foamy bile fluid rushed from his mouth. Striker shook his head and licked his lips refreshed and unfazed. He slowly, and methodically plucked all the embedded barbs from his skin.

The smaller guard bolted toward the door as Striker grabbed a tray and flung it into the back of the other guard's head nearly decapitating him.

The guard crashed through several pieces of equipment and flopped to the floor, unconscious.

The other guards rushed Striker, but he dispatched them with a series of blows in an adrenaline led total mismatch.

Zachary peered through the glass divider in disbelief.

Striker observed his imagined reflection and puffed his chest as if a major war had been won. "Savor the moment, for I am truly greatness." As Striker stared himself, his hallucination in the mirror exploded into thousands of shards.

Zachary's eyes widened. "I can't believe that this insane naked guy is making all of this happen."

Striker noticed the lab tech whose facial expression looked as if he was in the presence of Medusa and froze in place. He grabbed a nearby cart and slung it through the glass divider toward the lab tech.

As it crashes, Zachary's body blocked the Lab Tech to the ground before it nearly rendered him headless.

The lab tach lay in a puddle of his blood covered by the glass shards.

Zachary desperately searched for a safe place to hide until reinforcement could arrive.

Striker pranced in a circle, with purpose, up to one of the other prisoners. He studied his face intently as he smiled, and slowly caressed his profile. Striker drools as the inmate fascinated him.

Another Security guard blasted through an outer hallway door, snapping Striker out his trance. Striker enraged, snatched an IV pole, and shoved it through the inmate's chest which caused his heart to spew a torrent of blood everywhere including Striker's face. He licks the blood reveling in it.

Alarms blared as a code red light strobed illuminating the room pink.

Striker used the pole as a Samurai would a sword, jabbing through the next couple of inmates in a fraction of a second. He inhaled the smell of death and celebrated the rush.

Another security guard burst through the door aiming his revolver at Striker. He froze andtrembled in fear as he engaged a blood-covered Striker. The guard trembled in fear. "Hold it right there." His tone more of a squeak like a mouse than one in control.

Enraged, Striker marched right for the guard smashing obstacles out of his way. His eyes and anger fixated on the new prey. "I want you to die." When he reached the mousey guard, Striker snatched the guard's gun as the guard pulled the trigger, making it fire into the ceiling.

Stricker snatched the guard by his throat and lifted him off the ground as if to have superhuman strength slowly strangling him like Darth Vadar.

The guard thrashed within Striker's death-grip.

Strike enjoyed the moment and put his lips within one inch of the guard's ear. His stench of breath fanned the guard's skin. "I see what fear is!" Striker pressed his hands harder around the Guard's neck.

The guard tried to plead -- but gurgled instead.

Striker leaned in even closer and sniffed his prey. The smell was intoxicating to Striker as he savored the flavor to the point of ecstasy.

Zachary bolted into the room through the broken glass divider as Striker licked the side of the guard's cheek.

Striker roared like a lion and snarled at his reflection in a nearby mirror.

Zachary held up his hands to show they were empty in a non-threatening gesture. "Striker!"

The mirror behind Striker exploded as pieces of his head hit the back wall.

The guard Striker held, fell to the ground unconscious as Zachary stood shaking in his boots. As a trail of smoke oozed from the barrel of the security guard's gun. The guard heavily breathed as his chest rose and quickly deflated.

CHAPTER TEN

True Friends

Carroll's Delicatessen was not a typical New York-style deli. It was run down, but the food was to die for which kept the customers coming back. A cashier waited on Kevin and me to order. Kevin stood spaced out. I nudged him. "What are you getting?"

He jolted back to this planet. "I'll take a triple burger with cheese, extra fries."

I chuckled. "I Figured. Things never change."

It was always some dead animal for Kevin. I've tried to convince him to change his diet for the past twenty years, but he wouldn't have it.

The cashier wrinkled her nose at me. "And for you?"

"Veggie on wheat and bottled water."

Kevin smirked. "Still saving the planet, huh?"

"One of us has to. We all can't be a meat and potatoes guy."

We had this conversation many times. He always had the same witty response. "Everybody I know who eats healthy dies young. I hope you're not one of them."

I puckered my lips. "Now that is a new one. Are you trying to tell me something?"

"I'm just saying. Life is short; you need to live a little."

Kevin eyed the fry cook behind the counter. "Hey, Rocco, can we use your office?"

Rocco tilted his head to the left. "Yeah, sure, Kevin, anything for you guys."

Inside the deli's back office, Kevin ate and talked with his mouth full. "Snakebite is pretty pissed. He knocked me back to team coordinator for letting you out the lab."

I laughed with pride. "Snakebite?"

Kevin's demeanor changed, and I could see that he became uncomfortable because he knew the truth. "The guys I play cards with, call that son of a bitch a rattlesnake. You better watch him."

"I'm a little confused. Are you talking about Lynch?"

"I'm telling you."

I made a jazz-hand interpretation to mock my next statement. "Lynch makes me so scared that I'm shaking in my boots." Lynch didn't scare me. I've dealt with an asshole like that all my life. One more was no skin off my back. You had to find their motivation and fuck them over with it good and hard. That was my motto.

Kevin laughed as his demeanor postured into a defensive stance. "You should be. Do you know why they call him Snakebite?"

I re-evaluated the thought and slowly shook my head, clueless about the answer.

Kevin touched me on my shoulder as if I was his little brother. "Because anyone that goes against him, mysteriously dies in a freaking car wreck or something. You don't know whom you're dealing with; do you?"

I laughed at Kevin's interpretation of the situation. "Yeah, right."

Kevin let the situation sink in for a second. "Okay, let's think about this logically. Who's on board with our project?"

"What do you mean on board?"

Kevin lifted his brow. "Who can we count on?"

"Personally, there are only three people that I trust, me, you, and Abby. Everyone else at the lab is worried about their paycheck. Even you."

"That's because I have principles and don't have a trust fund, like you."

"Did you get me an appointment with Candies?"

Kevin stared at me, slowly shaking his head. "I'm afraid the answer is no. I thought you were a smart guy. This isn't about politics. Knowing Lynch, this is about money. We need to figure out who's being paid off. I don't want them to find you dead in a sewer pipe somewhere."

I tightened my jaw as my face turned red. "I don't care; he's not getting away with this; just set up the damn meeting for me."

"You sure?"

"Yeah! Absolutely sure."

Kevin looked at me for a second as he scratched his forehead. "Oh, that reminds me, I found that guy you've been hounding me about." Kevin handed Casey a note. "Here is his address. I've been told you need to be careful.

This guy is kind of whacked out. Do me a favor take someone with you when you go."

"What are you, my mother now?"

"Just do it."

I looked him straight in the eye.

CHAPTER ELEVEN

Meeting Moon

A mist covered my windshield as my GPS chimed in, "Your destination is on the right in six hundred feet."

I was unsure whether to continue my journey. The abandoned road was overgrown with six-foot-tall grass on both sides and a "Road Closed, Bridge Out" sign crossed it. My wipers scraped across my windshield, clearing the rain as I decided on what to do.

On the side of the road sign, there was enough room to pass it. Old tire mark showed that others had done it. I eased the accelerator as I squeezed my car around the detour sign and cautiously continued down the road.

I spotted an old single lane abandoned green metal with a wooden deck bridge just ahead. The bridge was on the verge of collapsing, and it looked as if built in the early thirties. Barricades covered the bridge with road signs.

"Your destination is on the right in two hundred feet."

"Siri, like I didn't know that. That's in the middle of the river. Where are you sending me?"

I was confused as I rolled toward the bridge.

"You have arrived at your destination. Your location is on the right."

I spotted the remains of an old driveway in an opening in the weeds. I turned onto the overgrown gravel road. At the bottom of the hill, my wipers revealed a multi-story dilapidated, dark and ominous abandoned mental hospital obscured by the overgrowth.

I glanced at the address, 355 Apple Grove Place, on Kevin's note, then back at the building. The only number which remained intact was the middle five. *This place is creepy.*

I cautiously pulled up to the building and scanned the structure; the building had no signs of life. I grabbed my hat and exited my car and noticed what looked like the main entrance and headed towards it. The place was five stories and looked as if it were built in the late twenties or thirties. The architecture was art deco and fabulous. The building had seen better days, and now it looked somewhat sad.

Years of old paint coats peeled from the entrance of the building exposing the gray and weathered wood behind it. I pulled on the partially opened door, but it didn't budge. I slowly squeezed through the opening.

I stood in awe of this once magnificent building. Shamefully, dirt and old equipment were strewn throughout. To my amazement, the interior was of another time -- the nineteen fifties perhaps?

A low growl came from behind me. I flinched and checked -- nothing. "Hello, anybody?" I heard nothing. I wondered if my dream world was starting to encroach into my real world again. It was hard not to let my mind go wild in here. I waited for a moment; then I took a step further into the building. I heard banging, which came deeper within the structure. I decided to follow the banging noise, which led me to a grand hallway.

I continued down the corridor, slowly and cautiously. I paused at the first open door -- a padded cell. I study it for a moment as I think. *Will I wind up in someplace like this*? I stopped in my tracks. "Is anyone in here?"

The strange gnarling growl returned as a pair of scrawny-white wolves crept toward me with their heads hung low, and hungered drools dripped from their gnashed teeth. They growl subtly watching my every move.

Without making any sudden moves, I tried to figure out what to do. I looked around and bolted down the hall that consisted of padded cells with rusty metal bars and crooked doors. This led to a partially opened double-gated bare passageway between corridors. I tried to slip through the gate, but it was too narrow to make my escape.

The wolves closed in on me.

I yanked the door again and tried to squeeze through. The wolves moved slowly closer. I finally squeezed through as one wolf lunged at me. The wolf's head stuck partially through as I yanked the gate closed-- it doesn't budge.

The wolf was frantic as I yanked the rusty gate again -- it only creaked as I put pressure on the wolf's head who was in attack mode.

I heaved the gate one more time, and the wolf howled as he pulled his head back and I slammed the gate shut. *Wow, that was brutal.*

I looked at the door and realized that I was safe from the wolves but trapped because both gates were locked. "Shit!" I looked for a way to open the back door. I tried yanking it to no avail. "Hey! Can anyone hear me? Is anybody here? Hel-looo?"

The wolves howled and snarled. They weren't pleased with my invasion of this building.

Shit!" I looked at my watch, and it was now 2:00 p.m. I heard a new noise. I realized it sounded like an old-time elevator.

The wolves disappeared quickly. Maybe they knew what was forthcoming. *What do they know that I don't?*

I heard footsteps headed my way. My jaw dropped as Cassandra Reid rounded the corner with the wolves in tow. She spotted me at the end of the corridor, and she smiled after she recognized me. As she inched closer to me, the wolves howled and snarled at me through the bars. I moved back slightly in the cell.

Cassandra whistled by placing her fingers between her lops. "Rocky, good boy. Milon, no! Go to your room."

The wolves were highly agitated, so they continued to snap.

Cassandra puffed her chest. "I said to your room."

The wolves slowly comply with her demanding tone.

Cassandra walked up to the cell door. "Those bars kind of suit you."

"I'm not amused."

"So, who's stalking who?"

"Oh yeah! This is a great pick-up spot."

Cassandra smiled, enjoying the moment.

I stepped forward. "I'm looking for someone."

"In here?"

113

I didn't feel like playing her games, so I remained motionless and silent for the time being.

Cassandra walked in front of the cell as her long nails clicked across off the bars. "Maybe I should keep you in prison for doing what you do. Maybe I'll just keep you as my slave."

I watched for a moment her antics trying to decipher if she was telling the truth or teasing me. "Moon. I'm looking for someone named Moon. Is he here?"

Cassandra stopped and stared at me for a long second before she answered. "He doesn't like visitors, especially unannounced ones. What do you want from him?"

I stared at Cassandra for a moment, wondering what to say. *What does she have to do with Moon I wonder? Is she one step ahead of me? She knew about D-214. What else does she know?* "What the hell, I need help with my research."

Cassandra laughed. "So, you want Moon to help you destroy people's minds."

"No, I want to stop destroying families because someone is in jail for thirty years and doesn't belong there."

Cassandra studied my eyes, and she must have heard the truth in my words. "Give me a credit card!"

Her words dumbfounded me as I furrowed my brow. "You'regoing to charge me to get out?"

Cassandra laughed again. "I should; you know what? Just give me the damn card unless you want to stay here all night!"

I complied as I handed her my credit card. She slid the card into the latch and slightly pulled the door. With no effort, her maneuver unlocked the door and popped the gate slightly open.

My eyes widened. "I'm impressed. How'd you did you do that?"

"I got a thing for locks; they can't keep me out."

"I bet they can't."

She thinks for a moment, then walks off down one of the halls. "This way."

I followed Cassandra through creepy halls. I had seen places like this photographed before. However, until you're in the middle of one, no photograph can compare to this vision.

We passed what looked like an infirmary, and the only item in the room was a baby carriage from the turn of the century. The place made my whole experience surreal. I almost expected a frightening clown to jump out from the darkness around a corner.

We entered a large, high ceiling room -- a grand foyer of sorts with massive pieces of highly unusual art. Oddly, string went from each painting to a center point. The lines looked like parts of cell neurons and dendrites. There was something familiar with this place. *Oh shit! It's Neuro art.*

The colors were a perfect match to my dream world. The whole room looked as if Salvador Dali painted the inside of my mind, himself. There was a painting of thoughts in the form of melted items everywhere. I became enthralled and fascinated.

I searched the paintings, and they took my breath away. I easily concluded that these pieces of art belonged to someone who had been here -- a special ability person who understood problems and my thoughts.

A voice from behind me broke my stare. "Like it, you do?"

That had to be Moon because it couldn't have been anyone else. He was what I pictured for the past several years -- a piece of art himself. He looked like an older Bohemian version of Cassandra, but not as well kept. The damn wolves flanked him. Thank God they were calmer but still vigilant as they snarled studying me.

"How are you doing?"

Moon continued to work ignoring me.

My eyes dart about the room. "This place is amazing."

Moon focused on one of the oversized paintings. He took a bucket of bright blue paint and splattered it across the canvas.

The super vibrant colors almost tried to pull me into my dream world. Suddenly, I realized he created his dream world here. I stammered in my speech. "Sorry for interrupting you, Mister Moon."

Moon stopped everything and turned his complete attention toward me. "No Mister. No, No, just Moon, Moon one name. Just one, no prefixes, no suffixes, just Moon." He spoke incredibly fast as if on speed. Instantly, he switched his focus again to switch back to his art.

I felt like a deer in the headlights, unsure what to do.

Moon squirted a glob of super vibrant red paint onto the tips of his fingers; and mentally tripping on whatever drug he took, the glob enthralled him.

I must admit, I was dragged into my dream world. Wow, this was new. I'm was right there with him.

He slightly opened and closed his fingers.

I mimicked his actions almost unconsciously.

116

Moon suddenly smashed the paint onto the canvas as if he conducted the colored paint like an orchestra conductor using his hands like a brush.

I suddenly understood what and why he did that. It was as if a fired off neuron hit my center brain. "Well, uhm, I'm uhm. Cas..."

"...I know who you are. You're Casey Palmer, you're thirty-two-years-old, and you attended Stanford. You're divorced, your daughter died, and head researcher for Clayborn Biomedical."

"Ex-researcher."

This fast-stopped Moon in his tracks. He smiled like a Cheshire cat. "Hum, that's interesting. Interesting indeed? A new fact for the day, to which I'm pleased."

I knew that voice, although the pitch was different, but, the cadence was the same as I had in my dream world. The only difference was that I had hundreds.

Moon switched his focus one hundred percent again and returned to his painting.

I think I understood how to talk to Moon; I needed to speak to him as I would Julie -- simple, direct questions. "I would like to ask you some questions about your experiments with your derivative."

Moon doesn't respond.

I looked at Cassandra. "Do you mind if we speak in private?"

Moon continued to ignore me as he wildly orchestrated his painting. Cassandra looked at me as she huffed. "This is as private as you can get. I'm not going anywhere."

Miffed, I stared at Cassandra for a moment but gave in. I focused my attention on Moon. "I'm having some problems with a new form of the derivative."

Moon stopped and rushed up to me. "Ahh, D-214 I take it. Yes, D-214, two fourteen, two, fourteen."

"Yes." I nodded to encourage him to keep speaking. I needed the answers that he could provide.

Moon inched closer to me. "So, did you meet the Devil yet; or, are you still with God?"

I swallowed hard caught off-guard by his question. I know what he was talking about, but I tried to hide it as "What do you mean?"

"You didn't think the further down the rabbit hole you travel, the lighter it wouldbecome, did you? No, no, no, indeed you're not that naive?"

Wow, everything he said hit home. It was like he saw into my mind.

Moon laughed and encroached into my personal space. "Hum? Are you afraid to answer my question, or are you afraid of learning the evil truth in your soul?"

Wow, this was super uncomfortable. It was as if he heard my thoughts and saw my visions.

Moon slowly ticked and jerked his head as if in a scary movie. "You never know what demons wait for these souls. It dependson the Devil's hold. So, how much hold does the Devil have on you." Before I could answer, Moon switched back to his painting. He grabbed a bucket of black paint and tossed it across his canvas.

Moon had a point that he clearly wanted me to realize. I pondered his words, especially those governing the Evil one crossing boundaries. "How can I stop the Devil's hold on me?"

Moon, wholly intrigued, approached me. "Ahhh, so you're there, I see. The true question has bubbled to the top, is that fear for you or me?"

His statement shook my inner core. It was as if he knew what I feared and planned on using them against me. Did we form a telepathic connection that diverse in nature?

Suddenly, Moon turned and bolted. The wolves jumped up and followed.

Stunned, I wasn't sure what to do so I tagged along behind him, and Cassandra followed us all through the halls of the hospital and up a set of stairs to the second floor. We traveled down a dark corridor and turned into a small room that used to be a small office. Moon headed to a large overstuffed chair and sat. The wolves sat on either side. The chair reminded me of my white overstuffed leather chair. We seemed to have the same taste.

Moon grabbed a pipe and filled it with a bud. Then he pulled out a small bag of powder and sprinkled it onto the pot, lit it, and took a substantial hit. "Time, time, time for one more question to me." The smoke filtered from his nose upward to the ceiling.

"Uhm, I need your help; I'm stuck."

"Stuck, you say. Hum let me ponder that in my dream. I will think of your problem and see what I can see." Moon sand back into his chair, and suddenly he's asleep.

I looked at Moon. "Are you going to help or what?"

Cassandra placed her hand on my shoulder. "He can't hear you now."

"Whatthe Hell. Now what?"

"Means he'll get back to you. He'll be out for hours."

119

Pissed, I walked off, and the wolves followed. "That's some bullshit!" I needed to know what to do. I felt as if I was so close to finding answers and not I faced another roadblock.

CHAPTER TWELVE

Time to Worry

Back at my house, I contemplated my meeting with Moon. The building of his mind-space disturbed me. It reminded me of the film *Close Encounters of The Third Kind* where Richard Dreyfuss' character, Roy Neary, can't get his vision of the mountain out of his head so he could understand it. I could see myself doing something like this. It was so apparent that he had some of the same visions me. I could have studied them for hours, never getting tired.

However, I had more significant problems I needed to address; specifically, the military projects use of D-214. If they started using it, problems would spiral out of control. I am sure they would blame me for the issues.

I grabbed my notes on D-214 and studied them as I walked about the house. The motion helped me think. I landed at my dining room table and continued to search through the notes. *It must be here somewhere.* I looked up and stared at the outside darkness. I pulled at my hair. *Come on, Casey you must find it.* I flipped the page and recognized an entry – "Tyler, twenty-fifth, 8:00 p.m." circled in red. I looked at my day planner and then the clock. "Damn, it's eight-thirty." I rushed out of the room head toward my lab.

At my computer, I typed – "HUMPTYDUMTY1" and hit enter. *WOW, I surprised my backdoor password still works.*

Images popped up as spinning icons. *That's new.* I click on one to saw a session in progress. I assumed it was Tyler's. I studied it for a second, and then I clicked on the brain scan monitor. I flipped between several different pages and changed my selection to the brain view and highlighted pituitary. The colors swirled on the monitor as the center of the pituitary turned completely black. *What in Hell is that? Did I change the color monitoring activity?* If not, this was a new pattern, and I hadn't seen anything like it. I typed in an old computer command. It pulled up a new box of values, and I studied them. Suddenly, my computer flashed thousands of red numbers. Puzzled, I paced and pondered. *What the Hell are they doing? This can't be sustained. Whoever this is must be going crazy.* I flipped back to the scan page and watched the monitor.

I paced, and a few minutes later, I headed to the kitchen. I pulled at the door of the fridge, but the door was stuck much like the rest of my day. I yanked the door open, and several items in the door fell to the floor including a syringe full of my red Neuro Confinement drug. I froze at the sight. I shook it off and picked things up. As I grabbed the syringe, I froze again. I looked at the needle and then glanced toward my computer. "Shit, can this work?" I raced back to my desk in the laboratory. I studied the images and the syringe. *Will it work?* *"Fuck it!"* I bolted for the lab.

I switched on several devices and climbed into my neuro bed. I quickly put on the neurolink helmet which resembled the laser device on the heads of the Neuro Confinement test subjects. The only difference was that mine was more advanced. I mustered up my courage and squirted the liquid into my mouth.

I looked at the clock on the wall -- 8:37 p.m. The second hand started to bang away inside my head as the second hand slowed, then the low murmured voices chorused. Suddenly, everything flashed to a blinding white light. The linking process began inside my mind to his. However, this place was vastly different. I stood alone engrossed by a complete whiteness of my dream world as the neurolink engaged. A small dark object appeared in the distance. I was hurled toward it at a blinding speed. I suddenly slammed to a stop, and the world started to fill in around me. A cinder block wall popped up, and then another.

As I began to move around in his world, I recognized Tyler. His eyes were dark and hollow and realized it was a representation of his soul. Suddenly, Tyler stopped and stood still in front of his creation, a hanging body which hung from the wooden ceiling. He stood in a protective mode as if on guard.

Tyler placed a knife onto a small wooden table littered with other deadly looking instruments. He seemed as if I was interrupted as he stared ahead past the inverted hanging man, on a sliding winch on a metal beam.

I suddenly found myself engulfed in Tyler's world -- our minds linked. My heart rate rose along with increased rapid breaths.

Tyler oddly smiled as if he didn't have full control of his lips. "Dr. Palmer, what are you doing here?"

Perplexed, I shrug frozen in my stance. *How can he see me? This is new.*

"The same way you can see me."

"Shit!"

Tyler gazed upon his creation. "Isn't he beautiful?"

I was unsure of how to respond. I contemplate a 'what if' in my mind and quickly asked questions and considered every possible outcome. I looked around and felt a nervous pit form in my stomach as the environment wholly transformed into a drab-earthed-cellar dungeon. Beneath the inverted hanged man, a fire pit glowed and gyrated in an eerie-orange hue.

Suddenly, Tyler grabbed a shovel off the wheelbarrow full of coals and resumed his chore and shoveled coal into the pit. He pumped a bellows that maintained the coal at a white-hot temperature as he smiled at me. "You told me I was going to meet God."

Tyler spun the hanging body around to face me and pushed it toward me. "Is this him?"

I was unsure of what to say and slowly back up.

Tyler noticed and decided to up the ante by picking up a knife and jabbing the point into the table.

I didn't like his behavior, and Tyler noticed he made me uneasy, so he started slowly twisting it back and forth.

I knew it was a game he chose to play. *What will happen if he pushes me? How far will he go?*

Tyler inched closer. "Are you going to answer my question or not?"

I stared at him. *What can I do so he doesn't know my thoughts?* The problem was he knew my thoughts – our thoughts.

Tyler enjoyed the banter flashing a sinister grin. He stabbed the table quicker and harder, driving the blade deeper. He twisted the knife back and forth a little faster as well. His breathing reflected his actions.

I realized he was getting off, and I didn't care for what was transpiring; it made me jumpy. I tried to keep it to myself, not knowing if Tyler could read my mind. I get my answer.

"Yes, I can." He smiled wryly as he challenged me by taking the knife, and lovingly started peeling strips of flesh from the victim's body. I had never seen anything like this before. It looked like a human butcher shop as cut-up body parts littered tables.

One wall in the room had two empty homemade prison cells. I spotted a pair of eyeballs that stared at me from beneath one of the tables. I noticed a severed head and assumed it must belong to the person he was carving.

Meanwhile, outside my house, Cassandra knocked at the door. Of course, I didn't answer. She beat on the door harder and, then, peeked through the window. She slammed her fist on the door. Still, no response, so she went around to the carport door.

***

In the dungeon, Tyler stopped and turned toward me, pointing the knife. "Are you here to punish me?" He waited for an answer, and I decided not to respond. He knew the

125

answer. Tyler spun the knife and thrust it into the hanging man using his body like a knife holder.

I relented after a moment and shuddered. "No."

Tyler smiled. "Good! I like you."

I decided at that moment that Tyler was pure evil, and I felt trapped. He was one of those that should never have been Neuro Confined.

Cassandra knocked on another one of my doors. Still no answer. She tried the doorknob; it's unlocked. She slowly entered. "Casey, you here?" There was no answer just the hum of my equipment which drew Cassandra in. She approached in silence, making her way cautiously toward the lab.

Back in the dungeon of the mind-world, the hanging man's neck seeped blood, and Tyler slit the middle of the victim's stomach. It looked like a failed attempt at an autopsy.

As the blood dripped onto the fire below, it stoked the coals producing a noxious smell. Repulsed, I choked back a gag.

Tyler noticed as he darted his eyes toward me. "You know, I've never shown this to anyone." He waited for a reply from me; there was none. He shrugged his shoulders. "My pets don't get to see it until they are selected; I guess this makes you special." Tyler looked down as he made a move toward me. He grabbed a knife from the table, and as he nears me, he glanced at me with a predator's smile across his face. "I like you; I had a feeling when we first met that you would truly get to know me." Suddenly, Tyler swung at me with the knife.

I stumbled backward as I block Tyler's thrust.

Tyler seemed amused at our cat-and-mouse game he would call slaughter. "You want to know about my pets, don't you?"

I looked for a way out.

Tyler continued to move closer as I back around the table keeping the distance between us.

"You can be my favorite, Dr. Palmer."

Tyler backed me into a corner, and I was out of options.

Tyler swayed waiting for an opening. Suddenly, he lunged toward me and caught my wrist.

I grimaced in pain. "Ah, shit that hurts!" Blood spewed forth everywhere, even onto Tyler's face.

Thrilled, Tyler seemed as if he was ready to jump for joy. "Oh yeah, now, that gets me hard." As Tyler gets off on the sight of blood, he licked his lips. Tyler took the knife and licked the blade. He took a small hand towel, and blood dripped from his wrist. He then wiped some of my blood onto the towel. He glanced down and then quickly back up. Blood dripped from his chin, creating a euphoric desire for me to taste it. I wanted to savor the salty taste as I ran my tongue down the blade with a slurp. "I guess this makes us blood brothers, doesn't it?" He lifted his bloody arm and knife not taking his eyes off me. "Don't worry; I'm gonna take my time with you so we both can enjoy this. You are special." He goes after me again.

Cassandra called for me as she rounded the corner in my house and saw that the Neuro Confinement programs were running. "Casey?" Cassandra studied the monitors for a second as the colors swirled the computer screens flashed as alarms blared.

"Warning, Abort in progress," drifted from the intercom. The Abort message flashed as the monitors showed my blood pressure and heart rate, which were off the charts. I seized on the confinement table.

Cassandra panicked, unsure what she needed to do.

Meanwhile, in Tyler's mind-space, I was locked in a struggle for the knife with Tyler. Tyler got on top of me with the knife inches away from my chest as his eyes glared upon me. "Dr. Palmer, you now get to be a part of me." He dropped onto the knife.

At the same time in my lab, Cassandra smashed the kill switch button and pulled the Neuro link wires and I.V. from me.

In Tyler's mind-space, the floor stretched as I sank into it. Then, boom! I returned to my white space. However, red blood spewed from my wrist. The blood was sharp crimson contrast to the pure white background. My inner voices fired up. *You must stop the bleeding in four-point zero minutes. Alternatively, you will bleed to death.* My inner voice started a countdown, louder and louder. It became almost intolerable. I started breathing heavy, and my pulse quickened. As I grasped onto my wrist to stop the bleeding, my inner voice seeped through. *"That will only slow the inevitable. You have three minutes fifty-eight seconds remaining."* Weakened, I dropped to one knee and became dizzy as I began to fade. "Fuck!"

***

Inside my lab, Cassandra searched for a way to stop the session. "Casey? Damn it." She grabbed her phone and dials Moon. The phone does nothing -- no signal. "Damn it! Shit!" She looked at my lifeless body, and then rushed out the front carport door and re-dialed. "Come on; pick up!"

Inside my lab, my head spun as I tried to steady my world. I was back in my lab. My hands felt like they were on fire. The pain was real, and I became drenched in sweat. I looked, down as blood spewed from my wrist onto the equipment. I tried to put pressure on my artery to slow the bleeding, but it didn't work. The clock on the wall pounded away, and I couldn't catch my breath.

I stumbled out of the lab toward the stairway. Midway, I collapsed and momentarily lost consciousness, barely alive. Somehow my inner voice engaged me. "Get up." I dragged myself along the floor using my sheer will power crawling up the stairs.

I heard Cassandra's voice from the carport. "What do I need to do next?"

CHAPTER THIRTEEN

I Want to Be with Her

I struggled to crawl as I gasped for air easing into my bathroom. I made it to the sink before collapsing. I tried to stand but couldn't. The ordeal with Tyler took its toll, and I knew it. *You have to fight back. How many times have I had to say that?* My body shook as I pulled myself by my fingertips against the rim of the white porcelain sink. I steadied myself as the room spun as the blood still flowed from my wrist. With my fingers, I reached for the water faucet, but I was unable to reach it due to exhaustion. I trembled as if coming off heroin. I slid back down to the under the sink and slipped into unconsciousness.

Cassandra rushed inside and rounded the corner. She saw that I wasn't there. Everything was the same as she left it -- except me. "Casey?" Only silence echoed back. She heard running water and bolted upstairs.

Inside my bathroom, the water filled the sink topping the bowl and spilling onto my lifeless body. As the water splashed onto my hand, it washed the blood away. The cut on my side also disappeared -- it all vanished. As I wake, I realized I was caught in a hallucination. Horrified, I slowly rubbed my wrist and hand. I took a deep breath knowing that none of it was real; it felt that way. That's what mind-space could do to your psyche. I breathed heavy and tried to collect my thoughts.

Finally, I pulled myself up to the sink and splashed water over my face. I lifted my head and stared into the mirror, and out of the corner of my eye, I saw something in the bathtub. Something clicked in my head. Oh shit! I recognized her. I spun toward her. "Julie!"

The bloody figure stared at me as she slid under the full tub of bloody water.

I freaked out and reached for her wrapping her with both arms. As I grabbed her, Julie became limp and lifeless.

Cassandra reached the top of the stairs and not sure where to go, she listened for a second and heard the running water. "Casey?" She headed toward the partially ajar bathroom door and then knocked on it. "Casey?"

The water flowed full blast as Cassandra entered the bathroom which was filled with steam. Cassandra scanned the bathroom and spotted me in the tub fully clothed, lifeless, and submerged. "Casey!"

She rushed to me and pulled my oxygen-deprived-blue faced body out of the water. She yanked me out the tub dropping me on the hardwood floor. She immediately engaged in CPR by hitting my chest. She felt for my pulse -- nothing. She counted to fifteen as she performed compressions, and then gave two breaths into my mouth as she pinched my nose closed. She hit me again and again. "Breathe; damn it!"

She continued with the CPR. After a minute, she checked his pulse; nothing. She turned him over on his side and slapped his back several quick blows. Nothing! She does another round of CPR and gives another couple of breaths.

Suddenly I gasped for breath as water poured from my mouth.

"That's it; breathe, come on."

I rolled onto my side and curled into a fetal position.

Out of breath, I struggled to speak, "You left, then your mom left. I'm so glad you're back." I grabbed Cassandra and pulled her close as someone would a child. "I've been trying to talk to you. Why did you run away?" I snuggled close to Cassandra. My brain thought she was Julie.

Confused, Cassandra frowned. "It's Cassandra."

I couldn't comprehend her. I sat up as rage overtook me. I blew a fuse and became furious. "I'm not going to let you leave me this time. I'm staying with you."

Cassandra slapped me. "What are you talking about?"

I couldn't believe that Julie would talk to me this way. I grabbed Cassandra and started shaking her. I decided to teach her a lesson and pulled her over my knee whipping her as if I was an upset parent. "I can't take it anymore! You're not going anywhere!" My anger was palpable, and I was furious as my arm flailed continuing to whip her.

Cassandra tried to stop me to no avail. Suddenly, she spun and wrapped her arms around me tightly squeezing me. As Julie evaporated, my eyes flushed. I slowly sank into Cassandra's arms. I cried as she held me; I completely broke.

CHAPTER FOURTEEN

Back to Normal

Cassandra cooked bacon and eggs as I entered my kitchen naked. I stopped mid-stride. "What are you doing here?"

Cassandra became perplexed and laughed. "You don't remember?"

I covered my privates embarrassed. "Remember what?"

Cassandra looked at my wrist.

How did she know about that? I unconsciously rubbed my wrists as I tried to hide other things.

Cassandra sighed. "Do you remember what happened?"

"I have no idea what you're talking about. I think I quit my job a couple of days ago."

"You mean fired two weeks ago."

"I think you're burning something."

The bacon began to smoke on the stove, and Cassandra lowered the heat. She gazed into my eyes, shaking her head in disgust, and then quickly turned to the stove. I bolted from the room.

After she prepared our plates, she placed them on the dining table. "It's time to eat."

I returned wearing my t-shirt and boxers.

"Thank God. I'm ravenous. You see, sometimes I go through spells of not eating for days, and then days of gorging where I can eat enough."

They sit across from each other at the table. Casey devoured the bacon.

Cassandra lifted her fork. "So, you don't remember anything."

I pretended not to hear her last statement and shoved a bite of eggs into my mouth. "This is good; you know how to cook."

Cassandra stared at me as I ate. "How long have you been hooked?"

"I don't know what you're talking about." I re-focused on my meal. "This is good. I wouldn't just say that."

"Don't play games with me!"

"I'm not."

"My dad's hooked on that shit, I know what it looks like. How long have you been on it?"

I realized she had been down this road before; so, I didn't answer. I took another bite of eggs.

Cassandra slammed her fork against the plate. "You're an addict!"

I stared at her as I poked my eggs. The conversation made me lose my appetite and took the wind out of me. I pondered for a second "What do I have to lose? It's how I conduct my research."

"I don't believe you."

"Believe what you want. It is what it is, and I can't change the truth."

"Who's Julie?"

I turned white, stunned. *How does she know about her?* "Nobody!"

"You're lying. She's all you've talked about for the last two weeks."

"I don't want to talk about her."

Cassandra stared at me for a moment clenching her jaw. "Finish your damn breakfast."

I pushed away from the table and noticed a pile of folders and other materials on the counter. "What are those doing here?"

"Those are my dad's notes. He said I should trust you, but I'm not sure if I should."

"Your dad?"

"Moon is my father. That's why you're not dead right now."

Holy shit! Now it all made sense. Cassandra had access to Moon's files, and that's how she knows so much.

Casey took a deep breath. "I don't think I've told you much about Moon."

"I already know a lot about him."

"He doesn't share anything with anyone. I don't know why he picked you."

I used his original research to make my first derivative. I think he was a genius. We went into two different directions but used the same base compound. Having met him, I think that we might be on the same path. At least we both seem bat shit crazy. I don't show mine to everybody. I heard he was a recluse so maybe neither of us do.

CHAPTER FIFTEEN

Evil Comes Calling

One of the most tragic person I had ever met, at least in my opinion, was Tyler. For whatever reason, he slipped through the cracks in Neuro Confinement. Tyler was pure evil to the core, but he hid it well. However, the program I developed weeded people like him out. The company placed profits above safety, and because of that, Tyler was administered the drug although he should have never been introduced to it. He was typical of what happened to psychopaths who were Neuro Confined which by all accounts was not a pretty picture.

A week after being released from Neuro Confinement, outside of his house Tyler played catch with his ten-year-old son. His residence was old and in need of a paint job as did his white picket fence. It looked like any middle-income house in America.

Tyler smiled as he pounded his fist into the worn-leather baseball glove. "Put it right here." He beat his fist against the mitt again.

The boy tossed the ball to his father.

Tyler zoned out as the ball passed inches from his glove. Tyler snapped out of it and pounded his mitt as if nothing happened. "Throw it right here."

His son laughed and pointed to the ball behind his father. "It went right past you, silly."

Confused, Tyler turned and saw the ball on the ground. He ran after it. The boy laughed again. "You're so silly, Dad."

Many psychopaths lived an ordinary life except when they involved themselves in their extracurricular activity. Everything seemed reasonable to them until they decided to do unspeakable acts. Neuro Confinement made those tendencies bubble to the surface, and as a result, they took their aggression out on others who were close to them and at the same time tried to protect those whom they cared. The massive dilemma was that they used the same strategy to confront their deep-seated emotional pain. Frankly, that could not work and created further turmoil and strife.

Imagine having thirty years to perfect your craft, but your craft was sadistic murder. How well could you get at hiding it?

As in Tyler's case, later that evening he was in the kitchen frying chicken legs as his son watched. He flipped a piece and grease splashed on his scarred wrist. "Damn it! Go get your mom."

The boy rushed from the kitchen as Tyler wrestled with the pain. He pulled and rubbed his burned hand to his chest. As he clutched his hand, his eyes twitched. A sizeable cooking fork dropped out of his hand. He seized but did not fall over. His eyes rolled back into his head as he had a micro seizure.

The boy and his mom laughed as they entered the kitchen. She froze when she saw Tyler. "Honey, you ok?" Panic filled her tone.

Tyler shook as the boy retrieved the cooking utensil from the floor, and then placed it on the stove.

Tyler gasped as his eyes bulged. "Stop! You're going to hurt yourself." Tyler trembled as he pulled the boy quickly away from the stove.

The fork hit the floor one more time.

In agony, Tyler's breath quickened. "Damn it!" He clutched his head with both hands and darted his eyes toward his son. "I've told you a hundred times to stay away from this stove! You never listen to me!"

Tyler's wife moved closer to him. "Honey, he did..."

"...Was I talking to you?"

Tyler's wife backed away, but not fast enough as he grabbed her and pulled her near. Tyler turned to his son. "Do you want to see what happens when you don't listen to me." Tyler grabbed his wife's hand and moved it inches from the boiling hot grease.

His wife realized what was about to happen and struggled to get out his grasp, which brought a smile to Tyler's face because he loved for his victims to fight back. She struggled to release her wrist from Tyler's grip. "Don't do it! Please, Tyler I beg you to stop this!"

Tyler slowly and deliberately brought his wife's hand toward the pan of grease. His breathing increased, and his heart raced as a maddening joy engulfed his face. He sneered at her. "I'm going to show both of you what happens when y'all don't listen."

Tyler's wife struggled more almost as if she could pull her arm from her body. "Tyler, stop, No! What's the matter with you?" She slapped Tyler with her free hand, but that had zero effect on Tyler's grip but intensified his anger.

Tyler tightened his grip on her wrist. "I'm teaching him a lesson." He thrust his wife's hand into the grease and held it there for seven seconds. He counted to himself. *One, two, three…*

She screamed in agony.

Four. Five.

"Dad, stop!"

Tyler glowered toward his son. *Six, seven.* "This is what happens." He showed his son his mother's cooked hand.

The boy shook his head from side to side in fear.

Then, Tyler plunged his wife's hand back into the grease as she screamed in agony. He repeatedly plunged her hand into the grease, again, and again. Her screams were music to his ears.

The pain caused his wife to lose consciousness.

Tyler's son ran and hid beneath the kitchen table, plugging his ears and closing his eyes.

A little later several police cars and an ambulance mounted outside Tyler's home. Three police officers escorted Tyler out of the house and shoved him into the back of a patrol cruiser.

The paramedics bandaged his wife's burn wound and then wheeled her on a gurney out the house.

An elderly lady followed with Tyler's son in tow and went to the back door of the ambulance. The boy looked at his father, who sat crazed inside the cop car.

Tyler mouthed the words, "I love you," to his son.

The boy was shell-shocked, and he diverted his eyes from his father.

Neuro Confinement tended to bring out many hidden secrets. However, many at the core of evil people should stay hidden or at least that was my humble opinion.

CHAPTER SIXTEEN

The Old College Try

IT was a Thursday night, and I was headed downtown to the library. Not all the files I needed I could obtain online; thus, the trip. I pulled up to a streetlight in the central business district. A girl on the other corner sold carnations out of a five-gallon bucket. *She gives me an idea.* The light turned green, but I sat pondering, and a car behind me quickly blew their horn.

I pulled through the intersection, and then I parked on the side of the road out of the way of traffic. I picked up my cell phone and dialed Cassandra.

"Hello?" Her tone seemed distant and soft.

"You still interested in a night out?" I held my breath waiting on her reply.

"I don't think so."

"Come on; let me surprise you."

Cassandra hesitated for three seconds. "I'm headed to class right now. I have to go."

I tossed my phone onto the seat next to me. An idea lit my brain. I smiled and carelessly whipped a U-turn in the middle of the road in traffic. I couldn't believe we went from enemies to friends the way we did. I wondered if there was some attraction between us. *I bet it would be a tumultuous relationship. God, why can't I stop thinking about her?*

I waited in my truck outside a downtown community college and waited for Cassandra to exit. When I saw her, I tooted the horn.

Cassandra crunched down to get a good look at me. She recognized me and flashed me an infectious friendly-glad-to-see-you smile as she strode my way.

I exited the truck. I held a surprise behind my back as I moved toward her.

She played coy. "Hey?" When she noticed I held something behind my back, she tried to look around me.

I never thought it would happen. I stumbled for words as I handed her three pink carnations.

Cassandra batted her lashes like a young schoolgirl in love. "What's this?"

I smiled as I averted her gaze. I couldn't believe I became shy. Timid wasn't like me.

She blew me a kiss. "Are you asking me out?"

"Depends on whether you say yes or not."

"Uhm... I'm not dressed to go out."

"You're dressed perfectly for what I have in mind."

Cassandra cocked her head to the side and took the moment all in. I could see the wheels turning, and then she took a deep breath. "Where do youwant to take me?"

"It's a surprise; I promise you'll love it."

"I don'tknow, I'm…"

I looked in her eyes. "Have I ever steered you wrong?"

Cassandra burst out laughing. "That's a loaded question."

"It's simple. You were there for me the other day. I owe you."

Cassandra reluctantly headed toward the truck. I was all grins as I helped her in and closed the door. I almost ran around it to the driver's side. I felt like a high school boy out on a first date. It had been years since the last time I took someoneout on a date.

We headed out of town. The countryside awaited as we tooled down a rural highway.

Cassandra stared out the window, watching the scenery. "Where are we headed?"

"One of my favorite places in the world. It's a surprise, remember?" We were headed to my happy spot. The place that I felt most at peace in this world.

CHAPTER SEVENTEEN

Time for Fun and Games

I slowed the pickup as police lights blocked the road ahead.

Cops directed traffic off the road and into a large field. I lined up with the cars and turned off the road. We followed the other vehicles into a large field, and soon I found a parking place. *I wonder how long it will take her to realize where we are.*

Cassandra was confused. She looked at me with a frown across her brow. "What is this?" She glanced at the people who exited their vehicles, and they were all families. She looked around and spotted a lighted sign -- "Gus's Traveling Carnival." She beamed surprised.

I smiled at her as I opened the door.

Cassandra teared up. "It's been years. The last time was with my dad. I was five or six."

"Julie was my daughter. She was six the first time I took her."

Cassandra teared up more, and she choked. "You're full of surprises. Wow, you're nothing like what I thought you were."

"What's that? Full of shit?"

Cassandra gets it. "I'm lost for words."

Gus's Traveling Carnival was a typical country carnival complete with a boardwalk filled with barkers and carnival games. The banners in front of exhibits looked as if they were constructed during the forties or fifties with many bright colors and oddities such as a painting of the snake girl. Just think, for a mere dollar I could see the only living half-snake-half-human on the planet or a two-foot-tall monkey boy who livedin the trees.

The boardwalk consisted of games of skills such as bank shot, ring toss, knock em dead, and many others. The prizes included large stuffed animals and small tokens of no real value. However, they became priceless relics that we cherished in our hearts for years.

Cassandra wanted to try all the games. I enjoyed the experience. Cassandra took a break after an hour of rummaging down the boardwalk and sat at a picnic-style table in the food court. I walked up toting burgers.

Cassandra finally dropped her guard and relaxed. "God, I needed this."

I was happy for the first time in a long time. "Glad I could help."

"I hadn't had a day off since I took care of my dad when he got sick for the first time two years ago." For a brief moment, a frown touched her lips.

I felt somewhat remorseful. "I'm so sorry for you."

Cassandra smiled at me. "It's okay. I'll survive; I always do." She gave me a look that she had fallen for me.

I enjoyed the moment and didn't want it to end. My mind raced with a myriad of possibilities. I needed to pull back for a second because I was getting way ahead of the game.

I needed to zap the moment and direct it toward my inner dreams. "Cassandra, ride the teacup with me."

"Oh, that is thrilling, if you're six."

"I have a problem with spinning things."

"Are you saying that you, Mr. Macho, are afraid of teacups?"

"I'm in if you agree to ride with me."

"Deal!"

"Teacup and the bungee jump, and then the carousel."

"I say bungy jumping and the roller coaster."

"Agreed; we'll ride every freaking ride."

We hit it off, and that day was one for the record books as far as first dates went. I was amazed by how fast our relationship progressed. I'm sure one of us would slam on the brakes soon as reality took hold. I hoped it wouldn't be me because she has a beau somewhere. *Why do we seem so comfortable together?* It's like we have known what each other thought and felt without speaking, which gave our relationship a mystical quality.

There we were strolling arm in arm as she ate cotton candy. She took a slow and steady deep breath. "I have to admit, not what I was expecting when you asked me out."

I pursed my lips as I thought about my next line. "It's not just for you; I also needed something to put my mind at ease, a little time to think. This is the one place I feel connected to Julie, my safe place."

Cassandra put her head on my shoulder as we walked. "Brings back memories for me, also." She fluttered her lashes.

I became extremely serious. "It's the last happy memory I have of my daughter alive."

"I'm touched. You're going to make me cry." We continued down the boardwalk. I became lost in my thoughts of Julie off in my dream world.

Cassandra froze when we neared a creepy façade. "Oh my God, a haunted funhouse!" She barely contained her excitement as she dragged me towards it. "Come on, we have to go!"

I laughed as she tugged my arm. "Those type of places scares the Hell out of me for some reason. I think it goes back to when I was young. I don't remember much, but images hit my consciousness from time to time, and I become quite shaken."

Several people made their way into the entryway of the funhouse.

They stood as a person in a Dracula outfit appeared from nowhere. One frightened young girl screamed like those in horror 'B' 1960s films. I admit that he spooked me. Then, he stood in front and center of the small crowd. "Welcome to my world!"

On cue, the lights went out as thunder and lightning filled the area. Most girls screamed. I did too.

Cassandra snuggled up to me as Dracula disappeared and a wall opened, revealing an eerie-dark-damp corridor.

I took the lead and grasped Cassandra's hand as we made our way toward the hall of mirrors. I stood in front of a mirror that made me appear short. I strode toward the mirror. The closer I inched, the smaller I looked.

147

"Cassandra, hey, I could pass for twelve. What do you think?"

Cassandra laughed. "That is whom I thought I was going on a date with."

"Oh, that's cruel."

We continued to a mirror that made us look fat. I examined myself in the mirror. "That burger did do a number on me. At least I'm not as big as you." I grinned, waiting for her response.

Cassandra playfully hit me on my shoulder. "You don't say that to a woman."

"No, but I said it to you."

"You did it now!"

I took off as she chased afterme.

As I disappeared in the darkness, I let go of her hand.

"Hey, where are you going?" Cassandra's tone was more playful than before.

I laughed. "Just follow."

I made it to a second hallway, which led to an infinity ofmirror illusion. A figure in the back went unnoticed fora moment. I noticed something move behind me, and it scared the daylights out of me. I whipped around, but no one was there. I looked back into the mirrors and saw Julie dressed in her favorite pink dress standing to my side. Blood started to seep from the side of her head as she reached forme.

Frozen by fear, I started to breathe fast. I quickly spun toward her; my daughter was in the mirror. No matter which way I turned, she was right next to me but in the mirror alone. That disturbed me. I started to freak out and looked for Cassandra. However, I am by myself. I gasped at Julie in the mirror. "Not now, Sweetie!"

That seemed to be a recurring theme with for my daughter. She became jealous whenever anyone, man, or woman, started to get close to me. She was very possessive.

As the artificial thunder cracked, followed by a lightning strike, I bolted down a dark hallway full speed stopping when I hit a dead end. I placed my hands on my knees and breathed heavy for a minute. I calmed myself down as a blacklight skeleton jumped out. I instinctively pushed him violently to the ground. The skeleton moved inches from my face; bones cracked. "Hey, watch it!"

What the Hell? A talking skeleton? I take off again.

I ran faster and faster until I reached a blacklight alien area. I slowed down again, trying to catch my breath, and just as I do, an alien grabbed me by the shoulder. I spun and decked the guy without even thinking. It looked like we played the knockout game with me victorious. At this point, I freaked out as my heart raced a million times a minute. My breathing matched in full-blown panic mode.

I made it to the barrel of love sliding to a stop. It was a rotating barrel with a swinging bridge rocking through the middle. The barrel slowly rotated. I froze and stared at it. My breathing increased, and I am terrified. "FU-K, I... I can't do this!" Real fear gripped me as my panic attack controlled me.

Cassandra laughed as she ran into me. I shook in my boots, sweating. She tried to get a grip on what was happening. "What is wrong with you, Casey.

"I... I... I told you I don't do spinning things."

Thunder and lightning manifested as another couple chased into Cassandra, knocking her into me with our lips only inches away. She leaned in for a kiss as I backed off.

I gazed into her eyes. "I… I..."

Cassandra grabbed me by the hand. "Come on, scaredy-cat." She dragged me across the bridge. I tightly closed my eyes and followed. Her touch slowed my heart rate as did my breathing.

CHAPTER EIGHTEEN

Time for An Update

There was a knock at the carport door of my house. I glanced at the clock; it's noon. I wore a T-shirt and boxer shorts. I peered out the window and saw Kevin. I partly opened the door. "I've been..."

"Are you gonna invite me in or what?"

I flung the door open as Kevin barged in. I'm still pissed from the other day when I got fired, so I wasn't exactly excited to see him.

Kevin headed straight for the lab. It seemed to call him like a homing beacon. He looked around the lab. "Wow, I see you've been busy." He spotted my new Neuro headset and picked it up. "I see you've improved it." He knew how to draw me in and made me forget that he pissed me off.

I stepped toward my headset. "I'm close, but still, I have a few glitches. However, I am working on a patch."

Who knows about this?"

I shook my head. "Nobody why?"

151

"Oh, I don't know, but I bet I could find one hundred and ninety million reasons to be careful."

I slowly took the headset away from him. "That's why I haven't told anyone." There was so much subtext in that statement that it worried. I tried never to show fear to anyone; especially Kevin. He would use it mercilessly on me because that was what he did.

I stared at Kevin, watching his reaction. I needed to know how serious he was with this. Kevin gulped. "I've got you a meeting with Candies."

I carefully observed Kevin's expression and body language. Something was out of place. "And?"

Kevin didn't want to answer and began to rifle through my workbench.

What are you holding back, Kevin?" I gave him a cold stare.

"You have a problem." He looked over his shoulder and moved close to me. "Somehow, Lynch found out about it."

"Somehow, I'm not surprised." I focused entirely on Kevin. "So?"

"Snakebite, remember?"

I moved closer with false bravado. "I told you, I don't give a shit what Lynch does. He could die in a sewer pipe for all I care."

"I'm telling you he's not someone to fuck with."

We fought like we were two rams who liked butting heads to see which would dominate. I never gave in, and Kevin never did either.

I continued to stare at Kevin. My phone rang from a text. I remained fixated as I walked away. "I don't care."

I looked at my text. "Cassandra, nothing yet." Thinking about her made me smile.

Kevin headed my way. "By the way, your buddy Zachary, got seven people killed."

"Abbey called me last night. I'm not surprised."

Kevin clutched me by my arm. "You have to stop this or more people are going to die."

"Wow, they fired me, and you want me to help them. Are you nuts? I could care less about what happens to the program."

"You know they are going to try and blame you somehow."

"I agree; that's why I wanted the meeting with Candies. He needs to see that I am on the right side."

"Candies will be a hard nut to crack."

"I've had worse. I think if I am straight with him, I'll be okay."

CHAPTER NINETEEN

Is This A Good Idea?

Senator Candies' office was what anyone would expect for a three-term senator furnished with overstuffed leather high-end furniture which exuded confidence and power. The conferenceroom was stately as well.

Cassandra and I sat like two lost pups in a wolves' den. Cassandra fidgeted. "You shouldn't have brought me with you."

I flashed a comforting grin. "I need you. Besides, you are the only one who can vouch for me on this."

Senator Candies entered and headed toward me. I was overly surprised that he seemed happy to see me. He stuck his hand out, and when he spotted Cassandra, he retrieved his hand; his demeanor changed. Senator Candies glowered at me. "Dr. Palmer, is this another ambush?"

"No, Sir, it's not. It's time for the truth to get out and the chips fall where they may."

Candies tightened his jaw as the veins in his neck seemed as they would burst. "Then why is she here?"

I glanced at Cassandra. "Because I asked her here, and she is the only other person on this planet who knows anything about this drug's side-effects that does not work for Clayton."

Candies stared at me as if we were in the middle of a Mexican stand-off. *Who will be the first to budge?*

Cassandra puffed air through his nostrils as if a bull.

I didn't budge and remained fixed in my stance. "I know you feel like I attacked you, but something has to be done, or people will die on this drug."

Candies stared for a moment as a frown touched his lips. "They already have."

"That's why I'm here. If you don't step in, there will be more. That's on you, not me."

"So, what happened in the latest incident?" Candies cleared his throat and leaned back in his chair.

"Senator, I only know what is reported on the news. I was kept out of the loop and fired, so I don't have access to any information."

"Are you kidding me? If this is going to be like the hearing you are wasting my time. I told you I would get to the bottom of this with or without you. So, why can't you tell me this time?"

"Because I'm no longer there! What do I know? They are trying to maximize their profits by bringing everyone through even if they are not a candidate."

"So, this is where the problems are coming from? Are you telling me they are putting criminals into Neuro Confinement that shouldn't be?"

"Yeah, but that's only part of it."

"Okay then, are you ready to tell me everything that's going on at Clayborn Biomedical?"

Candies was pleased that I was going to come clean. However, I started to feel like a rat. Something doesn't sit well with me. *Something is not right.*

Candies perked up. "You know what I need is proof."

I started to backtrack a little. I possess every file that they did and knew it might take years for them to unravel them all. A bit of paranoia kicked in. I sensed by heart rate increase and the shortness of my breaths. *Am I setting myself up to do time?* There were a lot of dead people, and I had to consider that Lynch would be thorough. *Would he be so bold to set me up for this?*

Out the corner of my eye, I glimpsed a black figure headed toward me. I instinctively raised my arm to block whoever or whatever was coming toward me. I flinched.

Candies took note of my odd reaction. "You okay?"

"Yea, yea, yea, it's just a fly or something." I breathed heavy. I decided I needed to get out of here. My eyes darted around. I moved toward the exit.

Cassandra stood and intervened. "We will get you something tangible."

I bolted out of the door. "This was a fucking mistake. I can't trust anyone but Cassandra."

Should I trust her? Is she playing me? My mind raced toward the deep end.

CHAPTER TWENTY

Finding the Evidence

Late night, in the Clayborn Biomedical parking deck, Kevin sat in his car as he shuffled through papers. He watched as a black Volkswagen Beetle as the headlights slowly faded off and slowly pulled into the parking deck and coasted to a stop. He slid down into his seat to obscure himself from view. Cassandra stepped out, studied her surroundings, and bolted to the building.

Kevin observed and then picked up his phone and dialed. "Guess who is sneaking into the lab?"

A little while later Lynch pulled up to the entrance to Clayborn Biomedical. It was late after hours, and the office building was dark and desolate. Lynch parked his car with his phone to his ear. "I'm at the office; I'll call you later."

I drove down the highway at about ninety miles per hour when my phone rang. I glanced at it and immediately answered. "Hey Cassandra, I was thinking about you. Where you at?"

"Did you know there have been fatalities in the lab?"

"Yeah?"

"At least thirty-five."

"Wait; what?"

"Thirty-five? Is that right? Does that include the seven from this week?"

"Is that mostly in the military lab?" Cassandra exhaled.

"Shit! I don't have any information about the military lab."

"It looks like these happened in the past two years. All in the military lab except two in your lab."

I was dumbfounded. "What, are you sure?"

"Yes, two were shot by guards, and it looks like at least sixteen committed suicide."

"Sixteen suicides? You've got to be kidding,"

"Shhh." Cassandra ducks low.

What?"

Cassandra lowered her voice. "Shhh. I've got to ..."

"Shit! My phone is dead." I pulled onto the side of the road.

The lights inside Lynch's office were off. Cassandra pointed her flashlight at an opened file on Lynch's desk. She snapped several pictures with her phone. Suddenly, several bluish video surveillance monitors captured her attention. On one monitor she watched as Lynch headed down the hall. She abruptly replaced a file. Lynch stopped at his door, reached atop his doorframe, and grabbed a key card.

As Cassandra started to leave, the doorknob twisted, and then the door opened. She tried to hide behind a filing cabinet next to the door. However, she obviously stuck out.

The overhead lights flicked on as Lynch entered and shut the door.

A janitor stopped the door from completely closing. "Sorry, Mr. Lynch, uhm, the new regulations are keeping us from doing our job."

Annoyed, Lynch flicks his wrist. "Put it in writing; I'll look into it."

"Okay, mister boss man, but your office..."

Lynch slammed the door on the janitor.

"...won't be cleaned."

Lynch headed to the filing cabinet, but Cassandra was no longer in that hiding spot.

He spotted a partially opened drawer. Lynch heard it as the door closed. He smiled and turned his head.

I was still on the side of the road, my phone was in the process of getting charged, and I was finally able to place the drop call back to Cassandra.

"This is Cassandra, leave a message." The phone beeped.

"Hey, we got cut off, what's going on? Call me back." Puzzled, I looked at the phone. *What the hell is going on? Where the Hell is she?* I slammed the truck into gear and peeled out, making a U-turn.

Lynch slowly strode over to filing cabinet, opened it, paused, and then glanced around. He closed the drawer, opened a second drawer, quickly grabbed a file, and then headed out, turning out the light as Cassandra's cell phone vibrated.

CHAPTER TWENTY-ONE

The Military Lab

The military laboratory treatment area was mind-numbingly expansive, and currently void of people. Confinement tables went on and on almost in a labyrinth stuck in infinity. In a surgical room, off the main confinement area, Lynch wrestled with Cassandra trying to buckle her onto a Neuro Confinement table. He leaned inches away from her face. "Who's after me?"

"What are you talking about?"

"Don't lie to me!" Lynch backhanded her across her face leaving red fingertip marks on her cheek. Cassandra flopped onto the table as Lunch continued to wrestle her. When she was in the position, Lynch buckled the last remaining constraints around her wrists.

She jerked and spat in his face. "You'll go to jail for this. Casey will find out."

Lynch's expression became demented and contorted. "You know, you are going to tell me everything."

"Fuck you, you filthy bastard!"

Lynch stood back and grinned as she struggled. Cassandra kicked and screamed at the top of her lungs as Lynch pulled out a needle filled with the D-214 serum. He held it up for her to see. "One way or another! I'm going to get it out of you. Is this what you were looking for?"

He stabbed Cassandra with the needle into her neck and slowly pushed twenty ccs of the Neuro Confinement drug into her vein. The dark blue fluid made its way into her veins and slowly spider-veined out to a bluish-purple. Cassandra seized violently.

"Wow! I must say Cassandra I rather enjoy watching you writher in pain. I might be a sadist at heart."

Cassandra's body continued to spasm.

***

I pulled into the parking deck inside Clayborn Biomedical, where Kevin sat waiting. As I parked, he stepped out of his car. "Casey, I called you when I recognized the car."

"Shit, I should've known she'd try something like this."

We rushed into the facility through the employee's entrance and headed toward the lab.

We burst into the laboratory, nothing. No one was there. The lab looked like it always did with nothing out of place. I glanced over to Kevin. "What about Lynch's office?"

Kevin nodded his head. "Let's go."

We raced through the corridors on a direct path to Lynch's office. Kevin was on a mission and reached the door first. He tried to open it, but it was locked.

My eyes widened, and I became extremely irate. "Watch out." I put my shoulder down and rammed the door bouncing off it and crumbling onto the ground. Lynch's key card fell off the ledge.

Kevin picked it up. "This might work." He slid the keycard into the lock. Click; the door unlocked. "Keeping that keycard, that is probably one of the most stupid ideas from Lynch yet."

I'm glad for his stupidity. "After you."

We cautiously entered Lynch's dark office.

I looked around. "I think she's been here." The office was in shambles.

"Oh, shit! Look, it's a small trail of blood."

I snatched my phone and hit redial. I listened as Cassandra's phone rang in the far corner by the filing cabinet.

"Listen, do you hear that?"

"That's a phone vibrating."

We followed the buzzing, and between the filing cabinets, I spotted a phone. "It's Cassandra's. She's been here, and now I think Lynch has her." I stooped down and fished it out.

"But where are they?"

I didn't want to think about it as my mind raced back to Kevin's quotes about Snakebite. My heart sank in fear for the worst possible outcome, and it would be all my fault. *Maybe she got away. Where would she go?* "Kevin, Let's go!"

CHAPTER TWENTY-TWO

Back to Moon

Kevin and I pulled up to the abandoned mental hospital. When we parked, Kevin's eyes widened. "What the fuck is this place?"

"Our only hope." I bolted from the car.

"Are you serious?"

"You know I don't bullshit! Come on; let's go."

"You want me to go into this place in the middle of the night? Are you out of your mind?"

"Yes, I am. Come on! We have to find out if she is here." Kevin searched the glove box and retrieved a flashlight.

We headed into the creepy building as I pulled my cell phone to light the way.

A growl followed us. Kevin stopped and slowly turned. "What the fuck is that?"

I hit the wall with my fist. "Shit, I forgot about the wolves!"

"The what?"

"Just keep up." I bolted down the hallway, and Kevin quickly followed.

I still had the sinking pit in my stomach. "Cassandra? Moon? Anybody here. Cassandra?" *God let her be here*. I rounded the corner and nearly ran Moon over.

Moon stood and brushed himself off. "What a pleasant surprise, Dr. Palmer. I've worked on the problem I have. I have, indeed."

I grabbed Moon by his shoulders. "Have you seen Cassandra?"

Moon ignored the question. "Follow me." He headed down a corridor as Kevin and I followed. Suddenly, the wolves stalked us from behind at a close distance.

Kevin cleared his throat and became unnerved as the wolves were just a couple of feet behind him. He walked backward, keeping an eye on them. "Could one of you tell me what is going on?"

I looked over my shoulder at Kevin. "Just keep up."

"Great. I don't have a good feeling about this."

We entered Moon's steampunk work lair. Everything had been recycled from the hospital and repurposed.

I looked around the room. "This is your mind space, isn't it? It's just like mine. Does it help you function in this reality?"

Moon doesn't answer; instead, he rifled through several files. "Your problem is D-214. Death, psychosis, schizophrenia waits this one; it's not good for everyone indeed. It fries their mind to the extreme."

I nodded. "I know. It affects those who are on edge."

Moon lifted a vial. "Those on the edge indeed. So, it is a good thing that I have an antidote. The only downfall is that it must be administered before they seize."

He handed me a large syringe with a big needle. I swallowed hard, almost a gulp. "Have you seen Cassandra?"

"What does she have to do with what I say?"

"Cassandra is missing."

"How can that be? I saw her at three."

"This afternoon?"

"That's what I say; I did indeed." Moon whistled, and the wolves quickly appeared. "Rocky, Milo, Luna, now!"

The wolves bolted sending Moon to follow.

Kevin punched my shoulder. "What the Hell was that?"

I didn't reply because my thoughts were on a dark outcome. My mind raced with every scenario played multiple times. I got a cold sinking feeling in my gut. Where was she?

CHAPTER TWENTY-THREE

Oh, Where Could She Be?

I sat in my home lab staring at the computer screen as I thought. I tried to sort everything out in my head. Kevin hovered over me, watching my every move.

Kevin scratched behind his left ear. "Where else could Candies have taken her?"

I shook my head. "I don't know."

"What would he do with her?"

"I don't want to think about it. He could have taken her anywhere!" Suddenly, I received a stroke of genius. "I got it. I think I can pull up where his badge has been." I typed into the search bar and hit enter. Different screens popped as I proceeded to decipher through a maze of computer commands.

"How are you doing that?"

I stopped and hit one final key on the computer. A new screen popped up. "The automated time system." I moved

166

through a few more computer screens and pulled up Lynch's login. It read:

LYNCH, MARCUS CLEARANCE TS-1.

Log in: 23:09:00 SECURITY CLEARANCE AUTHORIZED

TS-1.

23:09:01 UNLOCKED ENTRANCE 1-A.

23:11:32 UNLOCK DOOR 15-A.

23:12:45 UNLOCK SECURE DOOR 72-A

23:15:32 LOCK SECURE DOOR 72-A

23:15:38 UNLOCK SECURE DOOR 72-A

I studied the screen and then looked at Cassandra's phone. I quickly pulled up my call log:

CASSANDRA REID

TODAY

11:09 PM INCOMING CALL

11:11 PM OUTGOING CALL

11:12 PM OUTGOING CALL

11:13 PM OUTGOING

All the color drained from my face. "We have to go to the police?"

"And tell them what? That she broke into the lab and you think your boss has her? This doesn't show anything, and he tells them it's all your fault!"

The computer updated:

PALMER, CASEY

LOG IN 04:15:22 SECURITY CLEARANCE AUTHORIZED MS-1

The computer added another entry.

04:15:35 SECURITY CLEARANCE MS-1, UNLOCK M-1

Confused, my brow creased. "What the fuck?"

Kevin leaned in for a closer view. "What?"

"I just logged in." I looked at another screen. We watched it for a minute.

Kevin pointed wildly at the computer screen. "Lynch reactivated your ID. He's back at the lab!"

"Why would he do that? This has me extremely worried about Cassandra."

The computer added another entry:

04:16:32 SECURITY CLEARANCE MS-1, UNLOCK L-13.

I knew at that moment where Lunch was. "He's in my lab." I watched the computer with more updates as they started to scroll up on the screen:

04:17:01 SECURITY CLEARANCE MS-1, SESSION LOG IN.

04:17:12 TORTURE AUTHORIZATION CLEARANCE MS-1

04:17:16 RECONFIRMATION OF TORTURE MODE MS-1

***

Cassandra looked like she had run a marathon. As Lynch started the second dose of Neuro Confinement, Cassandra struggled to remove the constraints to no avail. "You son of a bitch!"

"Don't talk about my mother like that," Lynch was starting to toy with her. He liked this more than he should.

Cassandra screamed as Lynch injected more of the drug, she struggled and screamed as it dispersed, turning her veins purple once again.

Lynch huffed. "You could stop this at any time. Tell me what you were doing in my office. Who are you working for? Are you with Palmer?" He drew in a long-exasperated breath as he moved inches away from her face. "My patience with you is coming to an end. Are you working for that jackassCandies, Hun?"

Lynch whipped his face and smiled, intrigued. He watched her squirming as he injected the remaining dose. "It

169

won't be long until you tell me everything. Neuro Confinement has a way of doing that. That is if it doesn't kill you first."

"Fuck you." She spat in his face.

***

Suddenly I realized what was happening as my heart pounded against my ribcage. "Oh shit!"

"What are you oh shitting about?"

I was glued to the screen.

"What is Lynch doing?"

"Fuck! He's going to fuck me."

"What?"

I slammed my fist onto the table. "He's going to torture Cassandra and blame me."

"Can we stop him?"

My heart dropped. "We don't have time."

I spotted a syringe full of Neuro Confinement. I breathed heavy as I stared at the drug.

"Let's go!" Kevin bolted for the door.

I grabbed Kevin's arm and stopped him. "I have an idea. See if you can physically stop him. I'm going to try another way. Go! Go now!"

Kevin quickly exited.

CHAPTER TWENTY-FOUR

The Rescue

Inside my lab, I set up my Neuro link. I looked at the clock – 4:17 a.m. I took a hit of my drug and donned the headgear as I turned everything on. As the drug took effect, I am enveloped in bright white light almost blinding. I feel like I am nowhere.

Suddenly, Julie stood by my side, sweetly smiling. "I've missed you, Daddy." She bolted to me and wrapped her arms around me. She almost distracted me from my mission.

In the distance, a green dot formed and started twinkling. In an instant, my mind thrust toward the dot at breakneck speed. The speck grew into an empty cow pasture. The whiteness turned to a star clad black sky. The stars were so bright that I felt as if I could reach out and touch them.

There was something different about this world.

My voices began as a low hum inside this dream world. I wondered if I was in my dream world or Cassandra's. I spotted something in the distance. I walked toward it. As I do, parked cars popped up everywhere. I realized I had seen this place before. The cow pasture looked weird because the colors were so intense as the bright moon looked like a melted Salvador Dali clock bent over a tree slowly gyrating.

I realized it was the carnival. The colors of everything were super vivid, but harsher, darker, and spookier. The carnival was alive with motion but void of people as the colors pulsated in a weird rhythm. The festival was active.

Julie, smiling, waved for me to follow her. "This way."

As I meet up with her, she pulled me toward the haunted funhouse. I slowed my steps and tugged against her, not wanting to go, which caused her to loosen her grip on me. My heart raced as she ran ahead and disappeared through the doors. My fear was palpable. I shook as I trudged forward with my heart pounding.

Suddenly she popped back and waved at me to follow. "Come on!"

I made it to the dream world haunted funhouse and pushed the door open. I peered inside and slowly entered the blacklight colors, which danced and pulsated. The funhouse was a small living organism. I sank further into the haunted maze focusing on my goal.

A female scream pierced my inner droning voices, which caused them to stop; this had never happened before. It was like they recognized my fear. The walls slowly bulged in and out as if breathing. A gray alien in the painting started to move on the wall. It looked like it struggled to get out of the art. Suddenly the alien popped out coming alive.

The creature took in a deep breath for the first time in our oxygen environment. Relieved, the alien looked around and then focused his almond-shape-black eyes like a laser on me. I bolted down the corridor, and the alien chased after me. When I glanced over my shoulder, his long awkward legs that bent backward at the knee seem to lumber him for the moment as he gained his footing on unfamiliar ground.

Ahead of me, Julie appeared from around a corner. "Daddy, this way." She waved for me to follow as she disappeared through a trap door.

The alien's sloshing footsteps weren't far behind me; so, I darted after Julie.

Another scream pierced the air as I suddenly recognized the voice. It rocked me to my core. "Cassandra?"

"Casey!"

My name echoed in my head. "Cassandra?" I rushed toward Cassandra's voice. As I rounded a corner, a battle-ax nearly decapitated me as it swung from the darkness from above the door. I slid low as the ax came in for another try from the opposite direction and it missed me only by a fraction of an inch. I flipped up and bolted as the alien continued to slosh behind me. I knew I had to outrun the alien once again and stood hunched over with my hands on my knees, trying to catch my breath.

Julie appeared from another secret door in the maze. "Over here, Daddy." She reached out to me.

I took her soft hand, and she led me through several catwalks and tunnels. We exited through another trapdoor.

I bolted down the corridor as fast as I could. Until I reached the swinging bridge and revolving barrel, I came to a sliding halt. I stared frozen in fear. The alien's sloshing grew closer and louder as he chased us.

The Alien's looming shadow reflected on the wall. "Casey!" As he pounded the walls with the battle-ax, I slowly inched toward the barrel. As I do, it grew to ten times in length. I slowly inched closer to Julie.

"Daddy, hurry, come on."

"I'm right behind you, sweetheart." I had an extremely tough time standing as I moved closer to the churning tunnel. The spinning was dizzying and terrified to me; I swayed as the barrel turned. I wobbled and fell to my knees. I could not move forward. I struggle to stand, but it's like my feet were cemented to the ground. I am frozen.

The alien closed in as he swung his ax making his way toward me. "Casey, I'm coming for you!"

Suddenly I am hit with a thundering body blow. It's Julie; she has body-blocked me forward.

I closed my eyes, as Julie guided me through the black abyss landing hard on the floor of a torture chamber. I struggled to breathe. However, I slowly rose and noticed Cassandra strapped down on an old-time torture rack. It looked as if her captor had tortured her for a while.

Cassandra looked over at me; her eyes seemed as if they belonged to a china doll. Suddenly, I was propelled upward and hovered above her. "Cassandra!"

"Why are you doing this to me?"

"I'm here to save you."

Cassandra didn't believe me I could tell by the way she looked at me.

"You're killing me; Casey stop."

It hurt my heart to hear her plead. I never realized that I could care for someone so much as I did for her at that moment.

The rack clicked another notch as it stretched Cassandra even further. The horror that resonated out of my mouth shook me to my core.

A voice rang out, and it stopped me cold. I recognize it. "Tell me, are you working for the feds? Are they after me for the deaths in the lab?"

My voice rang in my head like a toothache. I couldn't believe it. It was me," or at least it sounded like me. I sank in despair as the reality hit me.

Cassandra screamed in agony again. "Why are you doing this? After all, I've done for you."

I couldn't get a grip on what was happening. *How can that be me?* I rationalized that I must be caught up in Cassandra's dream world.

***

Inside my laboratory treatment area, Lynch flipped a switch.

I saw through Cassandra's eyes as she glowered up at Lynch.

Lynch sneered and leaned inches from her face. "You are going to tell me everything. I need to know, or you are going to die!"

I noticed a rattling mirror behind Lynch.

Suddenly the mirror vibrated more intensely.

Lynch hit the switch, and then I was instantly inside my lab.

"Do you understand me?" Lynch spat as he spoke madder than a rabid dog having gone without food for weeks.

I focused more on the mirror's rattle.

Lynch reran the switch as Cassandra's body juddered in pain.

175

I screamed out as the mirror exploded into shards flying at Lynch-like daggers.

He ducked for cover.

"Oh shit!"

As a couple of them hit him in the shoulder, Lynch hollered out in pain rolling on the ground with his nose bleeding; he looked around and saw nothing.

The viewing room glass vibrated.

Lynch freaked as he ran and dove behind a piece of equipment.

The window exploded firing shards of glass again at Lynch. He looked paranoid as he slowly made his way to the hallway. He bolted down the corridor as the glass vibrated and exploded pummeling and lancing him, which resulted in hundreds of cuts as he stumbled down the hall.

***

Inside my home lab, my face distorted; the monitors gave unusual comprehensive readings. Suddenly, the computer screens in my lab vibrated as the brain monitor morphed to black. The EEG waves on the monitor became erratic, and they exploded one by one. I came to and attempted to grab the Neuro link. However, I didn't have enough strength to knock it off. I tried again and finally jolted it off my head, but the vibration wave grabbed me, resulting in a grand mal seizure. I turned blue as alarms blared. The energy wave controlled me as all the glass and mirrors exploded inside the military lab.

I found myself in a new dreamworld standing in a steaming shower surrounded by vibrant blue smog at my feet. I placed both hands on the glass shower door and leaned to see out. My hands slid down the panel leaving a crimson left handprint trail. I inhaled the warm blue mist deeply as I watch Lynch drag Cassandra's limp body off the Neuro Confinement table.

CHAPTER TWENTY-FIVE

Let's Find This Mother

Inside Clayborn BioMedical's high-tech lab procedure room Kevin tried to enter, but the security guard stopped him at the marked off with yellow crime scene tape. The shattered glass combined with blood looked like a nuclear blast that leveled the place. He noticed the empty laboratory table as he approached the guard. "Where is the guy that was on the table?"

"This is how we found it."

***

In the Black Roast Coffee shop, I typed away on my keyboard quickly bringing up the Clayborn Biomedical website. I typed in the security code, the site closed, knocking me offline. Frustrated, I took a long deep breath and waited for a moment before trying another code which kicked me offline again. "Shit! What do I have to lose? I'll use one of my old codes."

After I typed in the code, I was logged in. I opened a hack program and hit, "Run."

After a few minutes, Lynch's files popped up. I attempted a global upload. "Access denied; files too large."

A fail-safe severed the link. "Shit!" I slammed the laptop closed.

**

Later that night, I parked in a business parking structure next to the lab. I looked around and didn't see anyone. I exited my truck to grab a lab coat and cap and headed for the Clayborn Biomedical parking deck. I made my way to a side entrance.

With Kevin's security card near the scanner, I waved it across it. The door popped open, and I cautiously entered. With my head down, a hat on my head, I hurried down the laboratory hallway. I passed outside of a security camera's reach. In the hallway outside the high-tech lab procedure room, I snuck up to a six-foot tiered serving cart. I slowly inched the cart forward to investigate the viewing window, and peered in. Hundreds of patients filled the room, receiving the Neuro Confinement drug. Twenty or so workers hustled throughout the lab.

For a better view, I pushed the cart a bit. I stopped when I realized that D-214 bags of serum filled the cart. I peered back into the room and saw the two guards on both sides of the door armed with M-16s.

As a worker exited, I grabbed the cart I was hiding behind and wheeled it away. It left me completely exposed, so I quickly moved and hid behind the opened the door to the room as the orderly pulled the cart inside.

179

The door closed, and I continued.

I snuck to the hallway outside Lynch's office and checked to see if the door was locked. "Shit, it was!" I looked around and remembered that Lynch hid a crucial spare card on top of the door frame. I checked the door frame and found the keycard. With the keycard in hand, I tried, and it worked. Finally, I entered.

Inside Lynch's office, I turned on his computer and tried Lynch's password; it didn't work. I tried several other passwords, and nothing worked. Frustrated, I slammed my fist onto the desk. After a second, I took a screwdriver, and an SSD drive out of my pocket. I removed the computer case with the screwdriver and replaced the drive. I copied over a few files.

Someone on the outside of the door swiped a keycard and turned the knob. The door opened, and someone entered. All the office lights came on as I stared at the janitor. He caught me red-handed.

His eyes darted at the dismantled computer. "Good evening, Mr. Casey. I didn't realize you were still working. I'll go somewhere else."

"Thanks, Max."

The janitor left. *Fuck it.* I unbolted the hard drive out of the computer before it was finished copying all of the files, grabbed my stuff and bolted.

***

The sun slowly rose over the horizon as I sat slumped over in my truck in an empty parking lot in front of a bum-fuck Walmart. The hard drive was hooked up to my laptop by a bunch of wires which made it looked like as if I 'Frankensteined' together. A password hack dinged waking me. I rubbed my face and focused on the task at hand. I

180

typed in one of the hacked passwords, and the computer crashed. I rebooted it and tried the next password on my list. I tried several passwords in a row -- still nothing. I tried again; the screen ran different codes until a frame popped up with a smaller computer homepage on it. I smiled as I looked at the files. The program flashed off to the side, so I minimized the home page. The program flashed hidden files, which made me happy.

I quickly clicked on a file bringing up a surveillance video of a patient restrained to a bed receiving Neuro Confinement.

A female lab tech administered a large dosage of D-214 to Striker, and I watched in horror at the amount injected. Striker's veins distended as they turned purple. I could tell that Striker was hallucinating. Then, all Hell broke loose. My heart sank because I couldn't believe that this nightmare and torture to a human was something I helped create. Unfortunately, it was so far from my vision that it dumbfounded me. Dejected, I stopped the tape. I glanced at the next file of an Army sergeant who asked questions during an Army interrogation session. I slowly closed this file as well.

I stared at the screen for a moment, scrolled down, and saw a new unnamed file. I examined the date and froze when I recognized that this occurred yesterday. I clicked on it, and the file opened to surveillance video of Cassandra restrained on a Neuro Confinement table.

Instantly my heart sank as I watched her struggle with Lynch, who finally clasped the last restraint onto her. For me, it was tough to watch.

On the screen, Lynch leaned in close. "I told you, you are going to tell me everything." Lynch administered a large bolus of D-214, and Cassandra screamed as her veins turned purple from the concoction. I diverted my eyes from the screen because I couldn't watch Lynch torture her. I froze the image, again and drew in a deep breath before scrolling way further into the session.

I watched as Lynch interrogated Cassandra about what I knew, and then waited for a second before scrolling further into the recording. I stopped the fast forward when I saw Lynch administering to Cassandra another large bolus of D-214. She reacted like Striker; her veins turned purple, and she hallucinated, trying to grab with her constrained hands. Then, a violent rage overtook her as she struggled against the restraints. One restraint broke, and she freed her arm. She grabbed Lynch and yanked him toward her. He pulled away, ripping his jacket, which caused him to fall out of Cassandra's reach. She seized, grabbing her chest. I could read the monitor in the background as she flatlined.

Lynch attempted to resuscitate her, pulling the defibrillator paddles out and then injected her with adrenaline. "Shit, you can't die on me you, stupid cunt!"

I had enough and froze the frame recognizing that Cassandra had died. Lynch hovered over her with the defibrillating paddles.

My heart broke again. This was the third major tragedy in my life, where someone whom I loved was taken from me or left me.

CHAPTER TWENTY-SIX

An Ally

My truck was parked in a pretty rundown neighborhood. Saying it was the ghetto would be an understatement. I exited my vehicle wearing a heavy coat and baseball cap, which I turned back to trying to blend in a little. I glanced at my surroundings and made my way to a payphone. To my dismay, it was missing the receiver. I looked over at the next bank of phones; it seemed like one of them may work. I picked up the phone and heard a dial tone, and quickly slid a quarter into the slot.

***

Kevin watched an army guy who dusted for fingerprints and then swabbed the crime scene items in the high-tech lab procedure room. His phone rang, but he didn't recognize the number. He decided to answer anyway, "Hello."

I snorted. "It's me. I'm going to kill him!"

Kevin realized I was serious as he covered the receiver with his hand and made his way outside of the building. He strode to an isolated spot of the parking garage. "No one knows where he is; he disappeared along with Cassandra. Where are you?"

I didn't answer as I held my breath.

"Where can we meet in person?"

"Are they're looking for me?"

Kevin took a deep breath and paused. "You were logged in here. They think you did it."

"I have the proof; I have Lynch on camera administering a fatal dose to Cassandra. I have to beat him to the punch."

"I told you he was a rattlesnake. Didn't I?"

***

Lynch sat in an office with several other people. He pounded his fist on the desk. He leaned into a speakerphone. "I don't care what you think. Where is that son of a bitch?"

"I don't know. And, Sir, we also found a note. It says, tell Lynch, I know and soon everyone will. What do you think it means?"

"Just find him!" He grabbed the headset and slammed it down onto the phone.

One of the gentlemen next to Lynch bit the inner part of his cheek. "Let me handle it; it's mine now."

I grabbed the payphone again and dialed another number.

Abby watched television in her apartment. Her phone rang, she looked at the screen, but it had no I.D.; only a number. She picked it up. "Hello."

"You remember, hum, you remember where we built the kite?"

There was a long awkward pause from Abby.

My eyes squinted. "Are you alone?" There was another long silent pause. "I take it by the silent treatment you're giving me, you've heard."

"I've heard you had something to do with it."

184

"You know me, that's insane."

Abby took a deep swallow. "Thought I did."

Her words made me shudder. "I need to see you in person." The phone was silent except I heard the television in the background. "Are you there, Abby?"

Abby finally broke her silence with a sharpness in her tone. "I'm not comfortable with that."

"They killed Cassandra. Do you think you'll be any different to them? You know me; you have to trust me."

Abby again reverted to the silent treatment.

"Meet me there, inside in five minutes. You have to help me." I prayed she would accept.

***

Inside the military surveillance room, the place buzzed with energy. Agents traced the telephone calls on computers. An officer faced the others. "Get McAffe on the horn. I have it narrowed to a two-mile radius."

A soldier handed the officer a phone. "We have a lead on Palmer. He just called one of the lab techs -- a Miss Abby Grace."

Lynch rubbed his chin as he raised a brow. "Send me the coordinates."

The officer stood and faced Lynch. "You want me to pick her up?"

"No, let's see if she had something to do with it. Anyway, we may need her; so, let's get what we can out of her."

CHAPTER TWENTY-SEVEN

Home Sweet Home

My parents' house was a typical small-town suburban white picket fence wood-frame dwelling. However, it had seen better days since abandoned twenty years prior. Although the yard was mowed, the house looked in need of a few coats of paint. A car pulled into the driveway. Mist covered the windshield as the wipers scraped against it clearing it off revealing Abby.

Cautiously, she exited her car while glancing around. She headed for a partially open side door which was covered with plywood and pushed it open. She waited for a response that didn't come. "Casey?" Abby entered the house and slowly made her way to the center of the house in the dark. She watched from that vantage point. "Casey."

I stepped up behind her as Abby spun around. "Jesus Christ. You scared me to death."

"So, you think I had something to do with her death?"

"I'm, here, aren't I? Wait, how do you know about Cassandra's death?"

I stepped closer to her. Suddenly, I grabbed my head as pain shot through my brain, dropping me to my knees. My head pounded as if a jackhammer erupted my mind. I reached for the bottle of ibuprofen in my coat pocket. I unscrewed the cap as another severe pain bolted through me. I dropped the container spilling the medication all over the ground. I had to speak through my pain. "I watched Lynch give her a bolus."

Timidly she looked at me. "So, you were there."

I struggled to answer. "Ah, I have the camera files?" I pushed on the sides of my head to try to relieve the pain, but it didn't work. "God, I can't take this anymore!"

Abby became even more uneasy. She swallowed hard. "How did you know even to look?"

Another attacker hit me. I paused for a second and tried to compose myself. "Remember when we first started doing research, you said too bad you couldn't watch in real-time?"

Abby shook her head. "No, not really, why?"

"I thought about that for six months. I rewired the neurolink. In the last couple of months, I've been able to go into people's confinement sessions and become part of their dream world."

Abby's eyes widened. "What? You better start explaining this to me. And, that is probably the most stupid thing you could do."

"That's how I watched Lynch kill Cassandra. You could say I was there; sort of." I breathed heavy. "The footage on the security camera is in Pooky's hiding spot in the treehouse. It also contains Lynch's files about Neuro Confinement. He's paid off the prison board to get control

187

of the program. Please deliver it to Senator Candies. He has an office on Liberty." I struggled to speak.

A board creaked on the porch. I froze until another lightning bolt struck my brain.

Abby briefly closed her eyes. "Shit." Her word was barely audible.

I struggled to focus my thoughts. "I need to make sure that he gets it, no matter what. Please don't trust anyone. And, I mean anyone. You've always done the right thing." I studied her eyes, and then I grabbed my head and staggered for the basement door.

Two flash-bang grenades exploded, sending Abby dropping to the floor screaming.

Several soldiers battered through the door and flooded the room.

I tumbled down the cellar stairs. I tried to make my way through the cellar as I burst out the cellar door at high speed.

Lynch and two soldiers waited by the exit with their guns drawn. "Freeze!"

I put my hands up and surrendered.

Lynch walked up to me. "You're not that smart."

With my fists first, I flew into Lynch's jaw. A soldier jumped on me, but I became like a possessed man grabbing Lynch by the throat, trying to tear it out. A soldier's gun butted me, causing me to crumble to the ground. Another headache hit as Lynch stood holding his throat, coughing, with blood trickling from the corner of his mouth. "Palmer, you're going pay for this you little shit."

The soldiers quickly handcuffed me and dragged me away as Lynch spat out blood.

CHAPTER TWENTY-EIGHT

The Test of Wills

Inside Clayborn Biomedical medical high-tech lab procedure room, Lynch strapped me down onto the table with the help of several soldiers. Lynch beamed with accomplishment at this victory. "I have it from here, dismissed."

The soldiers vacated the area as Lynch prepared to administer the Neuro Confinement drug. "So, you going to tell me why you and your girlfriend were coming after me?"

"I know you killed her."

"How do you know that?"

"I watched you do it, you piece of shit."

"Did I ever tell you that you have a foul mouth?" Lynch retrieved a serum bag of D-214. "So, were you looking over my shoulder?"

"Something like that."

Lynch stabbed me in a vein. "I'm going make sure you suffer before you die, just for the fun of it." Lynch gave me a bolus of D-214. "I hope you can handle it better than she did. I didn't get anything useful out of her." Lynch sinisterly smiled.

I head-butted him. "Fuck you!"

Lynch grabbed his forehead as blood spewed. Bleeding, he hit the switch as I slung right into my dream world. He smiled as I writhed from the drug effects of being catapulted into my dream world.

***

I found myself standing in the middle of my parents' home living room. The furniture looked new, and everything had a shiny coat of fresh paint. My daughter entered and hugged me. "I just want you to know I love you." Julie smiled at me.

As she slowly strode away from me, I grinned. My arms jerked as I tried to release the constraints, but I froze in place.

Julie slowly trudged up the stairs stopping halfway. "Daddy, be strong." She turned and ascended the stairs.

Boom! A flash grenade exploded, filling the air.

The room immediately transformed into the old, dilapidated house; I looked up. A single drop of water hit me on the forehead. As I stared, the drip was followed by another, and another, until the house flooded. I gagged and choked as if Lynch waterboarded me, which made me think I was drowning. I struggled to move, but I froze in somewhere in a black glittered space. *How can something be so black, yet so glittery?*

***

Lynch hit the switch, which jolted me back into the bright white procedure room as I gasped for my breath. I tried to center my thoughts to fill my empty lungs.

Lynch coyly smiled. "So, how were you getting into their dreams? You're going to tell me everything, or you're going to die."

My world spun out of control. I couldn't get a handle on my location. It seemed as if all my blood boiled inside my veins as D-214 took hold of my senses.

"Palmer, I heard from your little slut that you can get into their dreams. How do you do it?"

I hyperventilated unable to speak.

"This is fun, isn't it? I can keep this up all night, Palmer. I must make sure you don't die first. However, you know what? I don't give a shit if you do." Lynch pushed a new round of drugs into my veins.

I tried to catch my breath. "I'll see you in Hell before I tell you anything."

Pissed, Lynch slammed the switch, and I seized.

***

As I juddered, I astral projected to the ceiling. I felt nothing. The world around me looked as if it was during my dream state, but not as vivid. I saw the evil little smile on Lynch's face as he enjoyed watching me suffer at his hands.

"You're already there. You won't last much longer, Palmer. You may as well tell me what I want to know. I can save your life."

I'd rather die.

Lynch hit the switch again, and again which plunged me deeper into my dream world and between my lab -- one after the other going in between both worlds led to a frightening yet exhilarating experience.

***

He hit the switch one last time, and I plunged me into glittered blackness which gave way to my incredibly distorted bedroom. I spotted the clock on the wall -- the second hand thundered to a stop melting into a puddle on the floor. The whole room brightened, almost too vivid, blinding me for a moment or two. Every item in the room pulsed as things expanded, contracted, morphed, and moved with each passing moment. I had only made it this deep once before. This was a version of my dreamscape that eluded me although it fascinated me. I headed toward my dresser, where Julie's image reflected in the mirror; however, she looked like a color negative. She moved as a trail of lights followed and quickly distorted into soundwaves.

I scanned the room, but she wasn't here. I looked back to the mirror.

Julie fixated on me with an intense-solidified gaze. "They don't like you. You must recognize that fact."

I'm taken aback by her words. "Who doesn't like me?"

Julie's eyes slowly rolled toward my bed as she tilted her head to the left.

I spun and spotted Cassandra who lay in my bed undisturbed.

"Daddy, they're coming; I can't protect you this time."

My heart raced as sweat beaded on my forehead. I turned back to Julie. "What about her?"

"She's almost one of us now. She doesn't want you here, either. You need to leave. I suggest you do it now."

I rushed toward the door. As I exited into a hallway, a couple of gangster types swiftly ascended the stairs. One held a baseball bat and looked as if he had been beaten to death by it. He slapped the bat in his hand and smiled. Splat! Splat! A very menacing sound if I ever heard one.

The other gangster was dark blue deprived of oxygen intake and had a noose around his neck. I took off toward the exit. As I went outside, there was no way down. I looked over the railing and decided to jump over and drop to the ground. However, the distance expanded from ten feet to twenty. As I moved closer, it continued to swell.

The gangsters exited the building and closed in on me. I hung onto the railing climbing down dangling as far as I could before dropping. I hit the ground and rolled, hoping it would help break my fall. I sprung up as one of the gangsters jumped to the ground. I took off the other way.

The second one jumped, reaching for me as I ran short of his grasp. I sprinted as fast as I could into a dark, foggy, street lit by an orange vapor light with them in hot pursuit.

The ground flexed slightly each time my feet touched the ground. As I raced down the road, I put distance between my attackers and me. I turned the corner as the street colors changed to a vivid urban color palette. Streetlights resembled lava lamps that pulled and stretched. This city was a living breathing entity. Ahead of me, a line of people waited to get into a club formed four deep.

I tried to blend into the crowd, but I stuck out from everybody else because my skin turned a unique sapphire color.

Eyes darted my way as I pushed through the crowd vying for a spot.

I froze when I bumped into Cassandra. She smiled at me, inches away from my touch. She started to kiss me, so I closed my eyes and turned my head slightly just as the end of a baseball bat rammed into my gut. Cassandra morphed into the guy with the bat.

I fell to one knee, the thug swung to whack me in the head, but I listed just in time. When the bat connected to the ground, the earth trembled rippling outward like a pond as if a rock skimmed across it. I pulled myself together as I bolted from the pursuit. I jumped like an expert parkour racer over a guard rail onto the street below. When I landed, the street rippled again quaking beneath my feet. I headed toward a row of abandoned office buildings.

***

Bam! Inside the procedure room, I was thrust back to reality as Lynch hit the switch. My eyes widened in fear, and I could barely catch my breath.

Lynch, amused, laughed in my face. "You ready to talk yet?"

I flipped him the bird although my wrist was bound. "Bite me!"

Pissed, Lynch hit the switch again. Bam!

***

I jetted back into my dream world and found myself in the Warehouse District. I bolted around another corner. I stopped, looked right, and then left. I looked back over my shoulder and decided to run downhill. At the bottom of the hill, in the middle of the street, several abandoned cars caught my eye. *Oh, fuck!*

In the alleyway, fire danced surreal inside a couple of steel barrels. Several homeless men gathered close to it to warm themselves as they watched me intensely. "What does a man like that have any business in this place?"

The toothless homeless man jeered at me.

"Just passing through. I mean no harm."

A heavy-set thug appeared from a shadow in front of me. He lit a cigarette as the smoke filtered toward the ominous purple and red sky that formed. I slowly turned around, ready to flee, but the street flooded with people. They multiplied at an alarming rate out of the shadows.

One of the thugs punched me on the side of my head. I spun and spat out blood along with several of my front teeth.

***

Inside the lab procedure room, I coughed up blood.

Bam! Lynch hit the switch again. I think he liked this game of his way too much as he glowered toward me. "What was that? Bite me!" Lynch laughed, enjoying the moment. "We must be getting to the good part."

Bam! Lynch hit the switch again.

***

Instantly, I found myself on the edge of a building overlooking the city. I faced several more thugs who held syringes eyed me. I knew the only thing that could be in the needle would take me deeper into Neuro Confinement. I edged carefully back teetering onto the lip of the roof, managing to maintain my balance.

They jabbed me everywhere with the needles. I fell backward off the building into a black spinning abyss. I slowly tumbled into the darkness.

I landed with a thud into an orange-rusty desert as far as the eye could see. Searing heat poured down onto my back as the sun blinded me. I soon realized that a strap came from nowhere whipping me naked. I lay spread-eagled onto the scorching sand as it whipped around me like a small tornado.

A large eagle circled overhead as if a vulture. The eagle swooped onto me as his talons dug into my flesh when he landed onto my back. The eagle pecked away at me as if my flesh consisted of birdseed. The pain echoed throughout my body and became quickly unbearable, knocking me unconscious.

***

Bam! I am back in the lab. Lynch spat on the floor. "I'm tired of this shit." He laughed as he pulled out a fifty-cc syringe and filled it with D-214. Lynch snorted. "I'm running out of time and patience." Lynch pushed twenty-five ccs into my I.V.

As I seized as my eyes rolled back into my sockets. My body became rigid, and I strained the straps. My muscles bulged as one of the straps loosened and began to tear.

Lynch moved close to my ear and didn't notice the strap breaking. "You're lasting a lot longer than I expected. I expected you to go quickly like that cunt of yours."

I became enraged and felt like Dr. Banner turning into the Incredible Hulk. I focused on breaking the strap as I controlled my rage to harness my strength like a laser beam.

The strap broke, which freed my arm. Now, I had my chance because Lynch leaned closer to my ear. I grabbed him by his throat and squeezed, letting my rage and adrenaline to do their job. I wouldn't let go of his throat for all the money in the world. He deserved to take his last breath for murdering Cassandra.

Caught by surprise, Lynch tried to speak, but nothing came out.

I focused on freeing my other arm and found success. I grabbed the needle in the I.V., jabbed it into the center of Lynch's chest and injected him with the remainder.

Lynch seized to my delight and entertainment.

I smiled as I released Lynch's throat. I unhooked myself from the confinement table as Lynch screamed in fear and agony.

Pure paranoia set in on Lynch as he pulled at his face harder and harder. He inserted his fingers into his mouth and ripped his face apart. Blood spewed everywhere as he choked on his blood. A grand mal seizure turned him blue, and he drew his final breath as foaming blood dripped from his ravaged mouth.

Unable to see and covered in his blood, I stumbled off the table. I bolted out of the lab and staggered into the hall.

CHAPTER TWENTY-NINE

Check the Freezer

I slammed into the wall halfway down the hallway and spotted a guard carrying an M-16 headed directly for me. He raised his weapon. "Halt!"

I collected myself and bolted into the morgue, banging the door behind me.

I knew the door didn't have a lock, so I glanced around the area for something to block the entrance. The guard reached for the door as I did. I pressed my body against the door to prevent him from entering.

The guard rammed his gun into the door. "Open the door!"

We struggled for control of the door. I spotted an I.V. pole as the guard back aimed his M-16. "I said, open the door! Now!"

I reached for an I.V. pole fingertip away from my grasp. *Shit!*

The guard yanked the door again. It jarred open a bit, but I pulled the door closed.

He rammed the door again. "I'll shoot if you don't open this door, now!" The guard lifted his M-16.

I stared at him as I grabbed for the I.V. pole.

With eyes of steel, the guard placed his finger on the trigger. "I am telling you that I'll shoot."

A banging came from the recesses of the facility.

I reached for the pole with my foot as the guard fired three shots into the bulletproof glass. I concentrated on the windows in the hallway behind the guard. The glass vibrated and then exploded -- one by one.

The guard dashed for cover as glass flew in his direction like bullets.

I reached for the pole as it flew toward me. I shoved it into the latch so the door couldn't open.

The banging continued as I drew a breath and realized the noise came from a nine-corpse stainless-steel body cabinet.

"Help!" The cry for help muffled by other distant sounds.

More banging and yelling from the corpse cabinet continued. "Somebody, help!"

It hit me like a ton of bricks when I recognized the voice. My strength faded with each second as the Neuro Confinement made its transition through my veins. *Am I just hallucinating, or could it be?* I steadied myself as I flung open a cabinet door. I saw something moving in the next drawer, so I quickly closed that door and started to open the next drawer. I dropped to one knee. "Cassandra?"

"Casey?" Her voice, although terrified, was music to my ears.

I gave out as I struggled to stand. I opened the door with barely enough strength to pull out the drawer. Cassandra lay wrapped in a blanket, so I unwrapped her like a present from Christmas morning. I kissed her, not wanting to stop -- several years' worth of emotions flooded between us. "Cassandra, I'm fading... struggling... I am trying to focus, but I'm losing the battle." I kissed her again and then helped her to her feet.

"I thought you were dead, Casey."

"I knew you were dead. Let's get out of here."

The backdoor flew opened as Cassandra, and I exited the building setting off the alarms.

Cassandra struggled to keep me upright. "Come on, Casey. Put one foot in front of the other, let's go. You can do it."

I blacked out.

CHAPTER THIRTY

In the Ditch

K evin drove on Highway 90 along the bayou with swampland on both sides. His phone rang; he recognized the caller. "Casey, where are you?"

Cassandra barely hanging on herself, holding me up, struggled to answer. "I need you... to come to get him."

"Cassandra?" The phone went silent but still active. She dropped the phone as she struggled with me. "Come on, Casey, you're going to have to help me!"

"Where are Y'all?" A splash on the other end.

Cassandra and I fell into the water.

A full moon illuminated the wind effect that moved the tall grass on top of an old drainage ditch. A wolf's muzzle pushed my face, but I couldn't respond. I felt lifeless but aware of my surroundings. I faded as time passed.

Sometime later, the wolf woke Cassandra by pushing his cold nose against her face. She wasn't in much better shape than me.

Moon rushed up to us and kneeled at our side.

Red and blue lights flashed as Cassandra sat in a large culvert rocking back and forth, as she held me.

I felt the wetness of my clothes and realized that mud covered me from head to toe but couldn't move. It was like I was Neuro Confined.

Cassandra shook violently as if she sat in a frozen lake during a blizzard.

A paramedic jumped across the ditch and stared at Moon. "How long have they been like this?"

"He's been in and out of consciousness for the last five minutes."

"What happened to them?"

"Don't know, not sure, wasn't there."

The paramedic waved toward his colleague. "Let's treat it like trauma; get a long spine board."

***

I tightly gripped Cassandra's hand. Inside my mind, I saw Julie. "Julie. I'm coming, sweetheart." Suddenly, I lay at the foot of the stairs at my parent's house. Everything pulsated, and the colors turned vibrant and brilliant with a Dahlesque ambiance. Outside the window, storm clouds rapidly formed. A murmur of voices chatted in endless waves. Heavy rain followed by lightning as a storm emerged. The murmurs became somewhat distinguishable. A person dragged Julie, ascending the stairs as she fought and screamed.

I watched from the corner of my eye. My breathing rapidly increased. My heart pulsed almost to the point of coming out of my chest. The voices became practically unbearable. I stood at the foot of the stairs looking up. Pow! A loud gunshot shattered the deafening roar of the voices which stopped instantly.

Nothing but the sound of silence remained as if in a black void.

I glanced up because I felt a drizzle of water drops landing on my skin, suddenly the sound of the drops thunder in my head as they turned into a torrent of blood pouring over the balcony covering me until I became a crimson red bloody mess. As the blood flowed freely around me, I slowly climbed the stairs making it to the top. The door seemed to expand to a vortex, but I was persistent and trudged toward it as if I wore gravity boots. The room began to spin.

Slowly, not knowing what I would find behind the door, I placed one foot in front of the other just like Cassandra once ordered. Something moved me forward, but I couldn't tell you what the source. I knew I didn't want to go. My life force started to leave me as I inched closer; the door flung open to a smoking thirty-eight revolver which lay in the hand of a twenty-year-old guy. He had no eyes; only black holes where his eyes should be. He looked at me with no expression at all. His face seemed like a mask. I lunge for him as he disappears.

Blood freely flowed over the top of the tub as I made my way to it walking around to the side. I stared at Cassandra under the red-colored water. *This has changed. I remembered Julie right there ten years ago.*

Cassandra reached toward my hand. As we grasped hands, images began. My life story flashed images so fast it was hard to concentrate as surreal; vivid memories encapsulated me.

I was in between worlds with one foot in the dream and the other in the here and now. My mind couldn't comprehend what was happening frozen in place like pieces of my dreamworld scattered amidst my reality.

CHAPTER THIRTY-ONE

The Final Hurrah

Inside the hospital emergency room, the doctors and nurses rushed to save me. The doctor barked his orders with authority. "Get neuro in here, stat! I need an EKG, bloodwork, and chest films. I'm not sure what we have people, but let's see if we can stabilize him."

A nurse raised her eyes to the doctor. "Pressure sixty-eight over thirty and a pulse of forty-eight."

"Let's get him in Trendelenburg. I need a pair of trauma pants."

I knew what that meant. A Trendelenburg position was where a person lay flat on their back, with their feet raised higher than their head the trauma pants squeezed the legs and abdomen so the blood could move to help feed the brain and raised the blood pressure. It was always a last-ditch move.

My mind spun in the different worlds. One second, I was here, and the next somewhere lost in a nightmare. Slam! I went back.

The doctor performed his task with speed and accuracy. "Put some trauma pants on him to see if we can get his pressure up. How far out is neuro?"

The nurse looked toward the clock. "They say fifteen minutes out."

"Let's see if we can get the drug here sooner; I don't know how long he can hold on. Where is respiratory? We need to intubate him now."

***

A new world opened to me. I saw my parents for the first time in a long time; both of whom were deceased. Also present were my dead aunts, uncles, grandparents, and friends. I spiraled into a heavenly spiritual realm. I felt a sense of peace consume me, and the voices in my head suddenly ceased.

I struggled barely holding my own. I rose above them and floated to the corner. I saw my silver cord this time and felt no emotions as wondered what I did to deserve this? I felt at peace.

I floated out of the E.R. room and to a stark and cold hallway with Kevin hovering over his phone like the angel of death. "Someone got to Casey. I'm not sure he'll make it. I've never seen anyone look like this."

I made out Senator Candies' voice on the other end of the line. "I'll make sure they will take care of him. I got the files. I pray he makes it."

"Me too."

***

Inside the hospital emergency room, there was no change as I relied on the life support machines. Kevin stared through a viewing window at the nurse. He mouthed his words. "How is he?"

A nurse shook her head just as I flatlined. The nurse hit an emergency call button.

Over the hospital sound system, a warning barreled down in the hall. "Code Blue emergency room two, Code Blue emergency room two, Code Blue emergency room two."

Despondent, Kevin's heart sank as he slid down the hallway wall.

**

In my mind, I transported to my parents' house at the foot of the staircase. I felt a rush as my life slipped away.

Julie stood next to me as she wiped her tears. "It's time to let me go, Daddy. This is not a reality."

"What do I have left to live for?"

Cassandra walked up to me carrying something in her hand. She smiled and nodded. "Not everything is what it seems." She slammed me in the chest with a larger needle.

**

I bolted upright on the emergency bed. I tried to breathe but fell unconscious.

Moon sat in the next room with an unconscious Cassandra hooked up like me to every machine possible.

The mood somber, but optimism seemed to take flight as my spirit world started to retreat.

An hour later, most of the chaos slowed, but the operating room looked like a war zone. I lay connected to the life support machines as my body rested in a higher Trendelenberg position. A set of shock trauma pants covered my legs.

CHAPTER THIRTY-TWO

The Hearing

The Congressional Hearing Chamber was filled to the brim with reporters and bystanders. The hearing was already in mid-session as the CEO of Clayborn Biomedical fielded questions from the congressional committee. Senator Candies presided. Journalists lined the chamber's side and back walls. Paparazzi snapped off pictures.

Senator Candies fired at CEO McAfee. "Mr. McAffee, how much money was allocated for Neuro Confinement?"

The CEO turned to his lawyer and spoke off the record into his ear who nodded. The CEO cleared his throat. "I'm sorry, Senator Candies, I don't have those numbers in front of me at this time."

Senator Candies pounced again. "Does five billion dollars sound about, right?"

The CEO turned to his lawyer for a conference. He looked at Senator Candies but didn't answer.

Senator Candies' jowls tightened. "Can you tell me why only one hundred and fifty million went to Clayborn Biomedical. How can that be?"

The CEO didn't answer, nor did he consult with his attorney.

Senator Candies blew air from his nose like a bull. "Where is the rest of the five billion dollars?"

The CEO didn't answer again.

Senator Candies started to stand but remained seated. "What happened to Dr. Casey Palmer?"

The CEO scowled back at Senator Candies. "I have no idea; I wasn't there."

"Did you give any orders to Mr. Lynch to kill Dr. Palmer?"

The courtroom instantly went silent.

"Again, I wasn't there. No matter how many times you drill me with your question, my answer is the same. I was not there. I cannot testify to something that I know nothing of."

The courtroom erupts in a mummer of voices. Senator Candies glanced toward the crowd. "Quite in the court."

The hearing doors opened as the crowd quietened; the paparazzi snapped photographs like vultures. Kevin and Abby pushed Cassandra and me in wheelchairs into the hearing room. Moon followed carefully carrying a large box of files.

The reporters sprang into action flinging a thousand questions to Moon who ignored them.

The CEO turned to see what the commotion was in the hearing and spotted the four of us. He turned white as mayonnaise.

By the look on his face, he knew the jig was up, and the truth would surface.

CHAPTER THIRTY-THREE

The Aftermath

I stood in front of an easel on a penthouse rooftop veranda overlooking the city. This city, to me, looked vibrant and clean. I think that day was the beginning of a new world for me. A world not limited by my addiction.

Cassandra sat with a coy expression as she gave a wink at me. I couldn't express the feelings I had for her because of the demons inside me. I couldn't scare her off. I needed her.

That was when I realized that I needed to stop and take it all in. I smiled at her. "The sun looks like a red ball of fire."

"It does. I've never seen it like this before."

"Look, it's almost at the horizon. The colors are vibrant."

"What's your favorite color, you see?"

"Not sure. I like the red, orange and purple with touches of blue and wisp of whites."

"I agree."

211

"It is almost as if Dali himself painted it. This was very much like a painting of my dream world. I think Moon had the right idea. You must get it out of your head, or it will drive you crazy." Cassandra snuggled up to me. "It's like therapy for me."

"God knows you need therapy."

They laughed as Kevin and Abby exited the penthouse onto the veranda carrying margaritas. Kevin drew a deep breath. "How are my two-favorite people?"

I nodded and smiled. "Better, it's been six months, and I'm clean. I've even slowed the drinking down."

"Sorry, I guess these are ours then -- more for me."

"Go for it."

Kevin laughed as he handed a glass to Cassandra. "Thanks, Pooky."

Not pleased, Kevin raised his brow. "Don't call me that!"

I glanced at my watch. "I wonder if it's on the news?"

Kevin sipped his drink. "What's on the news?"

Abby grabbed for the remote to the radio. "It's seven, and I haven't heard anything yet, either."

Kevin contorted his lips. "What are y'all talking about?"

Abby turned up the volume. "Here it is."

"Clayborn Biomedical's CEO Herman McAfee was found guilty of skimming billions of taxpayer dollars from a prison project. The company has filed chapter seven bankruptcy."

I grab the other margarita.

I raised my glass. "On that note, I think a celebration is in order."

Kevin gave me a questioning look. "Thought you quit?"

"I've slowed down; I didn't quit."

Kevin put his arm around my shoulder. "Does this mean we are out of a job?"

"I thought I would never say this to Rocky and Milo; I'm glad they found us."

Cassandra clung her glass against mine. "I'm just glad you're still here with the living."

"Me too. Can you turn up the volume?"

"In other news today a dozen former military soldiers from Afghanistan were found wandering the streets of New York. They seem to be suffering from an unknown type of psychosis."

I took a giant gulp of my drink, which caused me to grab my head with both hands. "This brain freeze is intense."

Cassandra bolted toward me. "Casey, your eye is starting to twitch, and your hands are trembling."

My body experienced a small seizure as I let go of my paintbrush.

Cassandra caught me and eased me to the floor. "Casey, you okay?"

"I'm all right; brain freeze, but with benefits."

Cassandra's eyes widened as she observed Casey's paintbrush painting on its own. "What the hell?"

"I've developed a new talent."

THE END.

A MESSAGE FROM THE AUTHOR

Thank you for purchasing and reading my book. This book was incredibly special to me as it was my first novel. Now that I have the bug for writing them, I want to share an excerpt from my next book, *Girl in the Mirror*, which will release on October 16, 2019, the day I have a guest-starring role on Chicago Med. Enjoy!

GIRL IN THE MIRROR

Sophie Marie White

Absolute Author Publishing House
New Orleans, LA

215

Excerpt

Chapter 1

THE RESTAURANT

A final burst of a busy Sunday brunch rush ended. I am Sophia or Phee as my friends call me. At twenty-eight, I'm taller than most women, lanky, and slightly muscular. With reckless abandonment, I plowed my cart through a pair of stainless-steel doors as if on fire craving to smoke my Eve 120 cigarette tucked behind my left ear. My dirty white apron matched my work ethic -- balls to the wall all the time. I knew my place, the bottom of the food chain, that was never any fun, and I always caught it from both ends, which I was forced to tolerate.

Like most working girls in the foodservice industry, I was over-worked and underpaid; but didn't care because my foot was in the door and at least I had a job. The same mundane thing happened every day -- I cleaned up the mess of a hipster crowd's fast-paced morning.

The place was on the order of A Court of Two Sisters in New Orleans but geared for locals and not a tourist trap. Marie's R'evolution, known for fine dining, provided a homely feel although each table was elegantly set with fine china and silver place settings on white-crisp linen tablecloths. Fresh-cut flowers, candles, and a small three-piece jazz band on the two-inch raised platform in the corner by the bar added to the ambiance.

New Orleans dining was more of an experience than just food; it provided a time for relaxation and a place where you always felt as if on vacation in an exotic part of the world. The atmosphere lent itself to patrons of the chic hangover crowd.

They sipped their spicy Bloody Mary's garnished with celery and garlic stuffed imported green olives while sporting Ray-ban sunglasses to cover their crimson streaked eyes. I hated it when a customer spat the olives onto the tablecloths as if cleaning them meant nothing to them. They were usually a fun crowd, but not on days like this where the night turned breakfasts into brunch lasting hours into the afternoon, and their demands were rampant. No matter what, I couldn't move fast enough.

Management abused me; mostly hated me, and the wait staff neither showed me love nor respect. They thought of me as if I were a lowlife that cleaned the tables, which was never fast enough for anyone.

The kitchen, a labyrinth of small, cramped, and tight rooms converted a hundred years ago from a wealthy family residence, left much to be desired in comparison to the dining area. With a twelve-foot ceiling and old-time ceiling fans that ran off a squeaking thick leather belt creating airflow in an otherwise hot, humid, and stuffy environment. It was neat and tidy, but undoubtedly a high volume, high paced place that if you snoozed, you'd never caught up. Long hours and shit pay were the norms just for the bus and dish wash staff. I couldn't say I hated my job because I needed one and at least here I was always free to be me. To be honest, I despised it.

I made my way to the sink, and then rinsed three feet of stacked dirty dishes alongside Miguel, early fifties of Mexican heritage. We worked well together like a well-oiled machine. I counted my lucky stars for this added benefit in an otherwise awkward situation.

Our manager, Spencer, mid-twenties who looked sixteen, burst into the kitchen wearing his hand-me-down grandfather's black Armani suit and a starched collared-white button-down shirt with a Flintlock teal feathered bow tie. Spencer was a piece of work because he tried to make up for his lack of manhood and height by bullying everyone around him, especially me for some unknown reason. No matter what I did, where I went, or the work I completed, he always looked for me to ride me hard as if I were his bitch. What else could I do but tolerate his behavior? It was either that or starvation.

I thought about stabbing him a couple of times, and I had enough opportunity but feared jail more. I can't forget the stench of his breath as it fanned my skin which always made me want to vomit. Sometimes in the lady's room, I did so I could remove his vile smell. Vomit was the preferred smell over his breath. When and if he touched me, his fingertips were coarse and scaly that I thought for sure he would rip my skin. Each time I shuddered from the inside out and let out a giggle to hide my true feelings. I know that I should have complained to top management, but I didn't want to be that girl. I'm not a troublemaker, and because he was the owner's grandson, it made things particularly more complicated than becoming a whistleblower to a sexual harassment situation. So, I tolerated him.

He entered the kitchen as I cleaned up the last dirty dish. When he gazed upon me, I felt his sharpness long before he spoke. "I'm docking your pay for last week's fiasco."

Miguel strode to the stove and began cleaning it to escape the upcoming barrage.

My throat pinched, and my blood boiled. "You can't do that; it wasn't my fault."

"I already did. And, make sure everything is done before either of you leave. You understand?"

"You're the boss." *No, you're a fucking asshole*. I flashed a thin-lipped grin and forced myself holding my tongue not wanting to get fired by him. I picked up the closest butcher knife. *I really should stab his ass*. I heard his speech so many times that I learned to ignore his ranting. I shook my head as I rolled my eyes. *I can't believe this shit is starting again.*

Spencer did stuff like this on purpose because he knows I needed to be somewhere else and he loved to simply fuck me without using any Vaseline.

"Excuse me, Spencer. I asked to get off on time today."

Spencer's face turned crimson red as he clenched his jaw inching toward me as if a bullet invading my personal space. "Remember, you need me. I don't need people like you." His spit splattered my face as he continued to wave his narly-little digit, which compared to the size of his penis must be pretty accurate.

Miguel looked over his shoulder and smiled at me as if he approved of my behavior. He mouthed, kick his ass, Phee.

My blood pulsed thundering in my ears as they turned warm and red. *Yep, I should kill him. That son of a bitch doesn't deserve to live.* I drew a deep breath as his harsh gaze knifed me. *He's such a coward. No, a dick.*

He flicked his wrist. "Well, are you going to just stand there?"

"Not exactly. I need to eat."

"On whose dollar?"

It was a stand-off for about three seconds when my eyes diverted to the water nozzle. I immediately went back to work, grabbing it as a weapon. *Oh, you have no idea what I'm capable of.* Water ricocheted off the pile of plates and spraying Spencer ruffling his feather bow tie. *Now you look like a drowned peacock.*

He lunged toward me, but the water outsmarted him as he fell on his ass, bumping his head against the stainless-steel prep table on his way down.

Miguel giggled as he scrubbed harder.

I leaned over him with a sly grin. "Are you okay?" *You son of a bitch, you deserved that and more.* When I'm pissed, I don't get mad; I get even. Well not really, maybe only in my mind. It was one of the reasons why I had been fired from several jobs. I didn't believe in taking shit from incompetent assholes with attitudes. "Ooops, I'm so sorry; the nozzle won't shut off."

219

Spencer attempted to block the barrage of water by raising his hands. He grabbed onto the preparation table, pulled up, and glowered at me. "Watch it, or you'll be out the door on your ass." He grabbed a rag off the rack and dabbed the water off himself. "Turn that shit off, now!"

"Okay, sure thing." *Asshole.* I took my time turning toward the faucet while holding the nozzle wide open. To me, this was me finally taking control and attacking him. Okay, I admit, water isn't exactly a knife stabbing, but under the circumstances it felt like it. Guilt encompassed my inner heart because I promised my significant other that I wouldn't get fired this time. I succumbed to his tyrant demand. "Yes, Sir."

As the water dripped from his suit, I slammed the nozzle against the side of the sink, pretending that it was stuck wide open. "I'm really trying Spencer. If you would have replaced the valve when I suggested maybe this wouldn't have happened."

He stormed to the sink and inspected the nozzle as I squeezed a little more. Water shot up precisely at the moment it needed to as his bow tie fell to pieces. *I wish I could kill him as easy as I did that damn bow tie.*

Miguel flashed a thumbs-up toward me, blew me a kiss behind Spencer's back, and then flipped him the bird.

"Shut off that damn water."

"I'm really trying." *Not really.* I grabbed and twisted the faucet as it snapped off in my hand. How perfect.

"That's it."

"Spencer, I think this is a job for you." I hand him the nozzle.

"Get out!"

"Well, what do you want me to do. Get out or finish the dishes? You can't have it both ways."

He shut off the valve perceiving victory.

Miguel approached the sink. "Do you two need help? We have been having trouble with the damn thing forever."

If looks could kill, both Miguel and I would be dead. I pulled my Eve 120 from behind my ear and slid it between my chapped lips, so I wouldn't mouth off pretending that it wasn't a good fuck.

"Your behavior won't be left unnoticed. I should fire you one the spot for what just happened. Go ahead, give me a reason too." He reached inside of his pocket and handed me his purple Bic lighter.

As I replaced my Eve 120 behind my ear, I shrugged off his gift. *Fuck you, not today.*

Spencer inched up, looked right in my eye for a long second, smiled, and then headed for the door. *Such a limp dick asshole.*

"You might want to try a different kind of bow tie, you know, one that can stay hard."

He spun back, his eyes widened in disbelief, and he pursed his lips almost choking on his spit. He shoved right up to me.

"My uncle sells ties on the corner of Royal." Miguel held his laughter as Spencer stormed from the kitchen without saying a word.

"Miguel, sometimes I dream at night that I have enough money to buy Marie's R'evolution. Oh, I'd have a revolution on my hands. The moment I can fire him, I'll show him what it's like to work for an asshole."

"You go senorita."

I loaded the glasses into the dishwasher, ready to explode. "I've quit better jobs than this fuckin hell hole."

Miguel put his arm around her shoulder like a father. "Don't let him get to you."

Tears flushed but suddenly stopped. "He doesn't."

"Bullshit! You can't bullshit a Spanish bullshitter. You change whenever someone gets under your skin." His tone and inflection reeked of his Spanish accent.

I ignored his comment even though I knew he was right to avoid crying because he acted and said things to me like I wished my father had. I took a deep breath and decided to pull up my big girl panties by attacking the dishes like no tomorrow. "But, he's such an asshole!"

"I got your back girlfriend. Spencer was more like a *Carajo*!"

Tightly pressing my lips, I grinned. "What's that, a dick-wad-bum fucking asshole?"

Miguel fatherly patted my back. "Worse."

"Fuck, Spencer. It's time for a smoke." I pulled my Eve 120 from behind my ear. "Give me a lite."

Miguel turned his head to the side. "You're just asking to get fired if you smoke that in here. Anyway, I thought you quit."

"Yea, yea, yea, save it for someone else. My doctor was all over my ass about it. She threatened to drop me if I don't stop."

Surprised by Phee's sharp tone, Miguel's brow furrowed as he took a deep breath.

"I'm sorry I didn't mean to snap at you. It's just he gets to me every time."

Miguel shook his head. "I got this if you need to go." He flicked his lighter to light my cigarette.

Do I, or don't I?

Miguel studied her facial expression as he patted the sweat off his brow using his sleeve.

I pulled back my unlit cigarette. "I'm almost done. It will take only a couple of minutes." I took the cigarette and placed it back behind on my ear.

"Couple of minutes? More like thirty."

"I know your right, but I need this job." I gazed at Miguel with big sad puppy dog eyes. I sped up loading the washer rack. At this pace, I was sure I'd break something.

Miguel gently grabbed my hands and stopped me from loading the rack. "Really, I've got it. I know how much you need to go. They won't wait for you." He began to load the dishwasher. "*Vamos*."

My ankle throbbed as I realized I needed to get off my feet. "Can we split our tips before I leave?"

"Of course. I wouldn't have it any other way."

I grabbed the tip jar and dumped the contents onto the counter, separated the money, and then handed Miguel a five-dollar bill from my take. "Give this to Rosa? I borrowed it."

Miguel tapped on his watch. "It's almost four."

"Yea, I know." I kissed him on the cheek like a daughter would kiss her father, and then dashed toward the door. Briefly stopping to look over my shoulder, I took a short breath. "Thanks."

"Have fun and don't get arrested this time."

I burst out of the posh restaurant's back door into the alleyway and headed to the street.

ABOUT THE AUTHOR

Sophie Marie White is a native of South Louisiana. She is married with three kids. She draws from her varied experiences as an actress, filmmaker, Director of Photography, Chiropractor, EMT, firefighter, race car driver, and boxing promoter to inspire her writing. She has been seen on television shows such as *Chicago Med*, and *Tell Me Your Secrets,* and in movies such as *We All Think We're Special* and *Hummingbird*. Her screenplays have won ISA New Orleans Writers Award 2017 and placed at Table Read My Screenplay (New Orleans, London, and Sundance), Final Draft Fellowship, ISA Fast-track Fellowship, and New York International Fright Fest. Her films have won or placed at numerous film festivals including AMFM, London Independent Awards, Imagination Lunchbox, and New Zealand Film Awards, Imagination Lunchbox and New Zealand Film Awards.

Sophie's next book, *A Girl in the Mirror*, will be published October 16, 2019, by Absolute Author Publishing House.

CONTACT THE AUTHOR

You can follow Sophie on her blog to stay up to date on her new releases, which includes her novels, television and movie appearance, and other things about her life. Be sure to subscribe.

Blog: https://www.sophiemariewhite.com

Email: Neuroconfinement@gmail.com